THE ALPHA'S BARGAIN (A PARANORMAL SHIFTER ROMANCE)

HOWLS ROMANCE

RYAN MICHELE

The Alpha's Bargain (A Paranormal Shifter Romance) (Howls Romance)

©Ryan Michele 2017

1st edition published: August 29, 2017

Editing by: C&D Editing

Cover Design by: Jessie Lane

The Alpha's Bargain (A Paranormal Shifter Romance)
(Howls Romance)

Dire straights.
Rock bottom.
Out of options.
It's where we were. My pack and I.
A simple bargain.
A childhood crush.

Could it work? In a world of fated mates how would we possibly fake it for everyone?

Luca made it all sound so easy. My heart, body, and wolf were on board. I just needed to convince my head.

I couldn't deny the alpha he was or the chemistry between us. Only time could tell if it would be for eternity.

A not so simple bargain changed it all.

CHAPTER ONE

THE WIND WHISTLED THROUGH THE TREES, BENDING the strong trunks to its will. Leaves rustled, creating music through the night's sky, while the clouds hid the moon, leaving everything blanketed in darkness. The smell of rain lingered in the air, indicating the storm was coming through hard and fast. Off in the distance, wolves howled, warning of the fast approaching weather change.

The air invaded my lungs, and the calm seeped deep into my body. My hair blew in the wind as the swing rocked back and forth while I watched the changes from my front porch. It was my favorite spot. Spending hours here had become my pastime. Whether the sun shone down, moon glowed, or the storm rose, sitting in this spot filled me with peace.

Storms were my favorite, though. The more lightning, thunder, and rain, the better. It was as if two worlds were colliding, bringing a force down on one another that rivaled the other. An epic battle of wills, crashing and tearing through the land—all of it part of nature and her works.

The clouds would sporadically give way to the crescent

moon playing hide-and-seek with the earth below. Small droplets began to fall to the ground, the dirt pressing out of its way before the water seeped in. A burst of energy floated through the air as lightning cracked, thunder crashed, and the rain began to pour down around me. All the while, not a drop hit me because of the large awning above.

Yellow eyes glowed in the distance, making their way quickly toward me. A beautiful, light brown wolf with white around his ankles hopped up on the porch, his nails tapping against the wood. He shook his body violently and fast, spraying me.

Rolling my eyes, I wiped the wetness from my bare arms and glared down at my brother as he shifted.

Ren stood before me with a wide, mischievous smile on his face. "Thought you could use a shower." He chuckled as a large crash of thunder reverberated, shaking the ground beneath us, my feet feeling the long rumble.

"And here I thought I liked you."

Ren reached down, snagging his sweatpants and pulling them over his body. Wolves never cared about nudity. It was a part of our lives, but being siblings, my three brothers kept themselves covered for the most part, which was greatly appreciated.

The swing gave a creak and groan as my brother's heavy weight settled beside mine, all the while the rain and wind picked up around us.

"Why do you love storms so much?" Ren asked, pushing the swing back and forth with his powerful legs.

Ren was the oldest and would one day be alpha, according to our father. A job Ren rolled with and didn't make much fuss about. Stating, *"He'd worry about it when the time comes."* Which was an admirable thing to me.

In some packs, rifts would cause problems between the

alphas fighting for dominance. So far, we'd skated those lines and hadn't had that issue.

"Peace, Ren. In all the chaos that is the storm, the peace will come."

He let out a huge sigh and laced his fingers behind his head. "Have you told Dad yet?"

My insides clenched, and the headache that stayed at bay began to come back, seeping into my temples. "No." Telling my father would mean trouble, and bringing that to my family wasn't on the top of my list. The problem was, it couldn't be hidden for much longer.

We were drowning.

Our pack, the one my father, his father before him, and his father before him had grown, was losing more money than we were bringing in. Therefore, our savings was dwindling to the point of scraping by, and no pack could survive the way things were. With sixteen mouths to feed, electricity that needed to be paid, and to simply live, we needed a holy grail of help.

I'd done everything possible to get us back in the black, and the stress of it was getting to me and my wolf. Lately, she was restless to a point where neither a run nor a hunt could calm her. The human side of me wasn't much better. The pressure of making things right, of helping my family and not being able to was sending me down a dark path.

It couldn't be stopped, because no matter what accounts money was shifted to or creative ways to put off the bills, they just kept coming. All of it weighed so heavily on my chest there were times I couldn't breathe and felt like an utter disappointment to everyone around me.

My parents had me attend the local Breed College and get a degree in finance, which only nailed my coffin harder, because I felt like a failure on so many levels. The problem was the money wasn't coming in as fast as we needed it, and it was time for everyone to get jobs outside the pack so we could get back on our feet.

Ren and I were the only ones who knew how low we were because I confided in him. It was either that or allow the pressure to take me completely under.

Knowing one day I was destined to be an alpha female, I carried the weight of my pack heavier than most. My natural instincts screamed to save the pack from all problems. Even though I hadn't yet had my first heat, my family knew my wolf, and I knew it, too. Eventually, everyone else would once I had my cycle, and then I would be more of a failure.

"We're going in now and talking to him, Caleigh. This can't go on, and the longer we wait, the farther down we'll go."

He was right. The only reason for me putting it off was my ego, which was totally stupid on my part. It was so damn hard, though, knowing you failed. You failed everyone around you when you should know exactly what to do to make it right. I had no other options at this point, and finding a money tree wasn't an option.

"Right," I breathed out, not wanting to, but having to do the responsible thing.

We rose from the swing just as another crash came to the earth. This time it felt like a warning, one that made the hair on the back of my neck stand to attention.

My father was the best man I knew—loyal, fair, and trustworthy to the highest degree. It was one of the reasons I was so down on myself about telling him. He had put so much trust in me to handle the finances, and here it was, all fucked up. Having him disappointed in me was the worst feeling ever.

Tears threatened to push their way to the surface, but I held them back while following Ren into the pack house.

"I KNEW we shouldn't have renovated." My father looked down at the papers on his desk, his hands feathered through his dark hair and his brow arched in worry. "That's what dragged us down so far."

He was right. Our pack owned two bars on the Breed side of town where the shifters resided. Each one gave a different feel to accommodate everyone. Howls was more upscale compared to The Grey Wolf where you'd find peanut shells all over the floor.

The Grey Wolf had been shut down now for four months for renovations that cost a mint. Alone, Howls could hold its own and then some, but with The Grey Wolf shut down and the amount of money going out to fix the place up, we were falling.

"How much longer before Grey will be open?" I asked, hoping beyond measure he'd say tomorrow. Hope was a powerful thing.

"We have about two more months." He rubbed his hand over his face and sucked in a breath. "Fuck, I don't want to go to the bank for a loan."

Breed had their own banks. That wasn't the problem. The problem lay in other packs deeming you as weak because you needed to take out the money and not have it on point. Nothing was ever kept secret, it seemed, and word would get out that my father couldn't handle his pack or businesses. It would create a rift and look bad on all of us. It could cause some to possibly challenge my father for his seat as alpha of the pack, which was a fight to the death.

"I'm so sorry," I whispered, feeling the ache in my chest grow tighter. The guilt of not hacking it rode me so brutally it hurt like a physical pain squeezing the life out of me.

My father's head popped up. "What do you have to be sorry for, Cal? You did everything exactly as it should be done. There are no I's undotted or T's left uncrossed here. You've done nothing wrong."

My words came out in a choke, hearing my father, yet still feeling like a disappointment. "I let everyone down."

"Nonsense. It's just more money going out than coming in. It's business, and you can't get all worked up because of it. I'll figure it out, Cal."

"What can I do?"

"Right now, nothing. Give me some time, and I'll get it worked out."

I had no idea how he would do that, considering we were more than a hundred thousand dollars in the hole after moving it from savings, but he's my pack leader and I put my trust in him.

My father rose from his chair behind his desk. "Come here."

I strode into his arms where he wrapped me in his warmth and kissed the top of my head.

"Next time, you bring this to me right away, Cal, and we'll figure it out."

I nodded.

"Love you."

"Love you, too."

CHAPTER TWO

THE GUILT STILL CLUNG TO ME LIKE STALE CIGARETTE smoke on clothes after a night at the bar. What my father had said was true, but I couldn't help feeling like I had failed in more ways than one.

"You know what you need? A night out! Let's go to Howls," my best friend Sage said from next to me as we lay on the bed upside down.

Looking up at the ceiling, nothing had changed. The fan still spun around and around, never stopping, just like life. No matter the ups and downs, it was never-ending.

"You do realize that, if I go there, that means I'll have to work instead of having any fun whatsoever."

Working as a waitress there wasn't a dream job by any means, but in our pack, everyone pitched in. While I did the finances, serving up drinks and bar food was also part of it. Not that I minded. Family was family, and we did anything for family. The problem lay in the fact that yes, by working there, I saved the pack money from hiring outside sources, but I wasn't technically bringing any new money in.

"No, you won't," Sage said, rolling over and looking me

in the eye, giving me the shut-the-hell-up look. "I'll make sure you just have fun."

"Sage, would you want to go to work on a night off?"

She shifted, moving the bed with her. "No, but I work at the bank. There's a huge difference." While this was true, she wasn't getting my point. "And you're down in the dumps. Like, majorly. What's going on?"

Sage had been my best friend since birth. We didn't belong to the same pack, though. Her pack was run by her brother Luca. They had been around for as long as we had, and our grandfathers had been very good friends; therefore, we were allies and looked out for one another.

The world had thrown many things our way, but the two of us had stuck together firmly. Even as close as we were, I never breathed a word about what was happening financially in my pack. Telling her would be a relief, even though my father now knew. However, Sage would set me straight. Maybe that's what was needed here—for me to be put back on the straight and narrow. A friend to tell me that I hadn't fucked everything up. A friend to listen and get all this washed off me, even for a little while.

Turning over on my side, I watched as my best friend's eyes widened in expectation. "This is just between you and me. Nothing goes out of your lips. Understand?"

"Got it."

Letting out a huge sigh, the story fell from my lips, including all my feelings of letting everyone down. She listened attentively, but her facial expressions were what caught my attention. The pinched brows, the running of her tongue on her lip, her eyes narrowing into slits—all of it told me so many emotions floating around that head of hers. All of which, for the first time since I'd known her, I couldn't get a read on.

Inhaling deeply, the words hung in the air like a cloak waiting to fall over us, heavy and thick, waiting for Sage to tell me what a disappointment I was and chastise me for not being able to handle things.

"Stop that shit right now," she demanded, sitting up on the bed in a rush, shaking it as I followed suit. "This isn't a guilt or failure thing. It's a you-don't-have-enough-money thing. Shit happens in life, and you deal and move on. Your father knows, so let him handle it. It's off your shoulders now." She made it sound so damn simple when it was far from being easy, quick, or without complexities.

"That's the thing—it's not. I'm still doing the bills and trying to finagle money around. The only difference is that now I have a little help, but nothing's changed."

"You're being way too hard on yourself, woman. But you always are. Taking on things that weighed your shoulders down that didn't need to be there. I know this is your personality, Cal, but it's time for others to help out. You can't fix everything."

She was right, but that didn't mean I had to like it.

"Forget going out. Let's watch movies, eat popcorn, and make homemade pizza."

A smile graced my face. She always knew what I needed. That was the perfect night for me. Sitting back and relaxing, and hopefully letting the world fall away, at least for a little while.

***

THE PACK HOUSE was huge and hadn't changed from the millions of other times I'd been to Sage's home. The place was enormous. Sage said once there were thirty-five bedrooms, but not all of them were taken, just room for expansion when the time came for her pack.

Tan stucco, the color of clay, covered the outside, while styled bushes and meticulously kept flowers lined the walls. The curtains on the rounded topped windows were open wide, letting all the warm sun into the place.

This had been my second home for so long I knew exactly where to park my Dodge Charger, and when I went to the door, I'd go right in like always. Normally, this was not a thing you did in another pack's territory, but for me, it was natural. Sage's pack had welcomed me for the most part.

"Hello!" I called out, stepping through the heavy doors that were taller than me by a couple of feet and gave a slight creak. Being five-foot-nine without heels was normal in my pack, but others, males especially, grew way above six-feet tall. Pack houses accommodated this with extended doors.

"You're here!" Sage called out from the top of the stairs as she raced down. They had one of those curving stair-cases, so when Sage came down, she looked like she was in a movie.

"I'm here. What's up?"

She'd called me right when I got out of the shower this morning, excitement bubbling off her. When she had told me to get over here, there hadn't been a chance to say no. It wasn't unusual to get a request like this from her, but it had piqued my curiosity and made me double time it here.

"Come." She looped her arm through mine and led me through the entryway, down the hall where pictures lined everywhere, and then stopped in front of another tall door. I knew what was behind it.

"Why are we going to Luca's office?"

Luca Ainsley was the obsession that never went away.

The older brother cliché of my best friend who I'd adored from afar for as many years as I'd been on this planet. He was also the man I stayed away from whenever possible because of said feelings for him and wolves were very physical beings. This was for self-preservation. So, standing in front of his door wasn't contusive to me staying away from the man. It was opening myself up to a world I'd tried hard to avoid for a very long time.

"Don't be pissed at me."

My glare came out as tension coiled in my gut. No one said those words without it being bad, and somehow, I knew. I knew what she had done, which had fury bubbling in my veins like hot lava.

"I trusted you," I whispered curtly. "You *told* him."

Not only would this look bad to other packs, it would hurt mine tremendously. My father and brothers were going to be pissed at me, and they had every right to be. I had told her because I needed a friend, because I had needed someone to lean on, and she had told her brother.

There goes, Cal. Fucking up once again.

"Please don't be mad at me. I thought he could help, and he says he can, Cal. I just want you guys to be okay."

"What happened to letting my father handle it? What happened to letting it go and letting him figure it out? Isn't that what you said to me two days ago?" I challenged as my temper got the best of me. I had a bad one and tried hard to keep it in check most of the time, but sometimes, it let loose and there was no stopping it. My father once said it was because of the auburn tint in my dark hair.

"I thought a lot about it. I'm worried about you. I know you. You're going to carry this around and drive yourself crazy to figure out a solution. You're going to lose sleep and not eat because your stomach will be all twisted up in knots.

You're going to have to let your wolf run more and more because she won't be able to take the stress. I want to help you; release you from this." Her face was filled with a concern I hadn't seen in a very long time. She really was scared for me, and I was scared for myself. In fact, I hadn't been eating or sleeping, and my wolf was clawing to come out. It would only get worse.

The anger began to subside, and I inhaled a deep breath.

"What is he going to do?"

She looked down at her feet. "That, I don't know. I just told him what was going on, and he told me to call you. You're here, and that's all I know."

"If my father finds out about this, I'm dead." Huffing out a breath, I closed my eyes and regained my self-control. I was here and needed to figure out what to do. Luca knew my situation. It was up to me to make this right.

"I'm going to kill you," I warned Sage, not that I actually would, but being pissed at her for a while was definitely in the cards. Even if it was out of pure concern. Confiding in her would be difficult next time.

She knocked on the door, the noise so loud it echoed down the hallway.

"Come in," Luca's deep baritone voice floated through the door like a melody. Over the years, it had changed so many times as he got older, but now, with its gruffness yet ease, it was the best. A sound that would arouse yet soothe. A very dangerous combination.

Sage turned the handle, pushing the door open. Luca's scent intensely hit me, and my attempts to not suck it in were lost. He smelled of fresh cut grass mixed in with freshly overturned dirt. Add in a huge splash of testosterone and his own unique flavor I hadn't quite figured out, it was delicious.

The alpha waves he threw off were a heady combination. My wolf inside howled, spun around several times, then growled in appreciation.

Boy, did everyone know it, too. Every female wolf in a thousand-mile radius knew of Luca intimately. He never hid it, because there was no point. He didn't have a mate and was a very strong alpha with a very high sexual appetite. There were many times I spent the night here with Sage, only to hear her brother with some female groaning in delight. It was one of the shittiest parts about having great hearing. If only it had an off switch when it came to blocking out that kind of thing.

Luca had become alpha when his father had become ill. Luca's father, Maximus, had stepped down, only to have Luca take his place. It was unheard of, but times were changing in the pack world.

Wolves were lucky in many areas, but with the mixing of shifter blood and human blood in some cultures, a very rare disease came into existence. It was a disease that shifting couldn't help heal the body. The doctors named it deliation syndrome, which was delayed revitalization, and since very few wolves had it, there wasn't much known about it. The pack doctors, though, had been researching it relentlessly and came up with a medication—another thing wolves were not used to taking—to help with the progression of the disease.

Luca rose from his chair behind the mahogany desk and made his way around it as I stepped inside the door. He was a specimen of epic proportions, standing over six-foot-five, towering over me. His dark hair was cut short on the sides, but the top had this messy just-got-out-of-bed look to it. The way he ran his fingers through it over and over again proved he didn't care much for it being styled in any particular way, only making it hotter.

His face was cut from granite with high cheekbones and a strong assertive jaw covered by a sexy dark beard. It was the eyes, though, the ones that made you feel as if he were looking down deep into your soul when he looked at you. They were a unique shade of brown, the irises gold that made them pop. At times, when he would turn, you'd swear they had a bit of green in them, too. I knew this because, growing up, I had spent a lot of time looking at this man, memorizing everything.

"Caleigh, thank you for coming." He propped his tight ass on the side of his desk, kicked out his feet, and crossed them at the ankle in front of him. His posture was relaxed and calm, allowing me to feel that way, as well.

He always had that way about him. Sage called it the calm before the storm. She swore he had a temper, but he'd never once showed it to me.

"Right, what can I do for you?" I clasped my hands in front of me, waiting for him to lay whatever this was on me so I could figure out a way to save face with my pack.

His lips tipped up in a sexy smirk, then fell when he looked at his sister. "Go, Sage."

"I want to stay." Sage crossed her arms over her chest, trying to give off that don't-mess-with-me vibe, but she never won. Not ever. Not once since I'd known her.

"Go," he ordered again, to which she huffed and turned to leave.

"I'll be outside the door," she told me, pulling the door open.

"No," Luca called out. "Leave us be. I'll have Cal come find you when we're done."

Sage narrowed her eyes at Luca, and his face became stern, his body giving off strong alpha vibes that had my wolf up on her feet, at attention. The bitch always liked those waves.

Sage lowered her head and left the room without another word. A room that now had Luca and I alone. Heavens, I lost my damn mind being in this confined space with this man.

"Let's cut right to the chase. I have a bargain for you."

CHAPTER THREE

My hands felt fidgety, so I stuffed them in my jean shorts pockets to try to tame them. That didn't help much, just gave them a little bit of cover.

A bargain. What in the world could this be? I had nothing to give Luca, so my bargaining chips were already spent. There was nothing to bargain with.

"Look, I know Sage told you what's going on. I'm sorry that she put that on you, but I don't need any help. My family and I will work this out. I'd appreciate it if you wouldn't say anything to anyone about it."

Luca sucked his lips between his teeth then released them with a small pop. He gripped the side of the desk. Everything about this was cool and calm. "You got yourself into a mess, it seems."

"And I'll get us out of it," I snapped a bit too harshly, because his alpha waves hit me fiercely, but I kept my shoulders straight and stared him in the eye. This was mine and my pack's livelihood here.

I'd been around alphas all my life, including my brother. Yes, he could give off massive waves, but that didn't mean

I'd put up with his shit. Learning how to handle them had become a must in my life.

"And how are you going to do that?" he challenged with a gleam in his eye.

That knowing gleam had been there once before when we were kids and he told me worms in human form were just as good as in wolf. Having the crush of a lifetime on him, I had believed him. He'd been dead wrong.

"Luca, don't play with me. I don't know yet. The answers haven't presented themselves, but they will."

"What if I could erase all the debt and give your family cash, would you be up for it?" He rubbed his chin as he focused his attentions on me, breathing in and out slowly.

A laugh billowed up from low in my chest. "Right. Are you going to head out back to the money tree? Because I can tell you, those don't exist."

His smile made my breath catch in my throat. "Yes, as a matter of fact."

"Luca, did you bump your head?"

His laugh was deep and sexy rough, one that I'd missed since avoiding him over the years, yet this one was deeper. "Quite a few times, but it has nothing to do with this."

"Okay. So, say you give me all this money, what is it that you want in return?" There was no way Luca would do this out of the kindness of his heart. We might have known each other for years, but that didn't constitute shelling out this kind of cash to bail us out.

"That's the best part."

Something in his tone had my back straightening.

"You."

My hand flew to my neck as a reflexive gesture. Over the years, it had been a gesture that only made its appearance when the situation made me seriously shocked or surprised.

"Me? What about me?"

"I pay the debt, give your pack the money it needs to get afloat, and the payback is you coming to live here with me for six months."

"You're not serious. You want me to sleep with you? Like a prostitute?"

Luca had never shown any interest in me that way. Sure, we had the catty back and forth, but never sexually on his end. Yes, I had a few fantasies, but him, never. Not even a look that would suggest it. This was so far out of the blue, it was in another universe.

He rose from the desk and stalked toward me, eyes intent and jaw set in a hard line. "You would never be a prostitute." He placed his hands on my arms, sending shards of tingles down them. "This is a mutual agreement between two consenting adults."

"But why? Why me? I don't understand, Luca." And I didn't. Luca could and had had every woman around these parts, except for me. Maybe that's what this was—a chase or something he thought as unattainable. He just wanted to notch me off his bedpost.

He moved his rough hands up and down my arms, sending more tingles in their wake. "Time will tell this. But the bargain stands." The pause between us was seconds yet felt like hours. "I want this, Caleigh."

Luca dipped his head down, his beard brushing my face and kissed me intensely, rough, and with so much passion inside of it I felt lost. So lost I gripped his shirt to hold myself down to earth before I floated away to another universe as I kissed him back.

He tasted of mint and chocolate, just like my favorite ice

cream. Our tongues did a little dance together, each move-ment almost choreographed, like we'd been doing this forever and not for the first time. Luca sucked the air from my lungs, and my heart beat so fast I thought for sure it would leap from my chest.

He pulled away from me and only then did I slowly open my eyes.

My lips felt as if they were stung by bees, leaving behind a tingle. When I looked up, Luca's eyes were molten, showing more of the golden rim, telling me he had felt that passionate kiss just as much as I had.

"Wow," I whispered more to myself than him.

He smiled at hearing my breathlessness.

"Six months. With me, here in my house."

"I can't let you pay my family's debt, Luca. It's not right."

He brushed his nose against mine in such a caring way it was a shock. No man had ever given me that tender of a touch. "If I can have you in my home and in my bed for six months, I'll be a happy man. I want this, Cal. What if I wired the money into your business account? No strings to me?"

"And what do I tell my pack? Oh, I just had a hundred-grand pop up? That's ridiculous." Even entertaining this idea was absurd, but with his heat so close to me, my brain couldn't function normally. My body was on red alert, and my wolf paced back and forth, growling. She loved this idea.

"I had a feeling this would be a hang up for you. Do you remember Ivan?"

"Of course." He'd been a pack mate up until a year ago when his body had given out. He'd been hundreds of years old, and it'd just been his time. His death was had been felt throughout our entire pack hard.

Luca gave me a squeeze, then released his hands from my body, leaving coldness in their wake. He moved back just a bit to where I had to bend my neck to look up.

"We are going to say that he left your pack a nest egg. It's been caught up in litigation with the Breed Counsel and has just now come to light. The sum will be given to your father as a lump sum payout. All the legal documentation will be there. I will put the money in, and no one will be the wiser."

My mind reeled. This man had thought of everything. The Ivan story would work because he'd had several stocks and bonds that we were able to get. This money could go into my pack clean, without anyone knowing what I'd done. All for six months of time with Luca.

"But, why would I all of a sudden pick up and move in with you and your pack? That doesn't make sense."

He reached down, taking my hands in his, then lifting them up to his lips, planting a soft kiss on the top of each, then holding them to his chest. "You tell them we're mates."

I gave my hands a tug, but he didn't let go, holding them fast. "I can't say that! One, they know I haven't had my heat cycle; therefore, I can't have a mate. Two, what happens at the end of six months? I put my tail between my legs and crawl back to my family? You know there's a possibility they won't take me back because of this."

That thought made me want to throw up. Being a lone wolf wasn't on my agenda for life, and that would be exactly what happened if Luca tossed me out and my family wouldn't take me back. Would he use me then throw me out?

My knees began to buckle, and I gripped his hands that he wouldn't release for support at the agony of what this could do to me hit full force. A female wolf's dream was never to be out in the world, alone and desperate. Those wolves were forced to do many things they didn't want to do to survive. Some changed into their wolves and never turned back into human form. That wasn't the life I wanted.

Heavens knew what my family would think. They had every right to not take me back into their fold after the six months, but if they found out I lied, who knew what they would choose.

Luca leaned in, rubbing his nose against mine, then pulling back. He had a serious thing for it, and it gave me serious tingles throughout my core each time, along with sending shivers of calm throughout me. "Your family will take you back after the six months; I'll make it so. That isn't an issue. As for them not believing the mating, it doesn't matter. As long as you come to me of your own free will, they cannot do anything about it."

Even growing up, Luca had been seriously smart, excelling in pretty much anything and everything he touched. Him having the answers so calmly shouldn't have surprised me in the slightest, but to have it this planned out on my behalf did. He'd always been a thinker, examining all the components of situations before acting. It was what made him an exceptional alpha. At least, that's what my father always said about Luca. They worked closely together.

"I can make all your pack's money problems disappear today, Caleigh. One phone call and it's all finished. I won't force you to sleep with me, Cal ... ever. If that ends up not being a part of this, then so be it. I just want you."

The weight on my shoulders felt too much to carry. With what I had done with the money, and now this ... it was all too much.

With one bargain, it could all be erased. My pack wouldn't have the burden. They could get all the renovations done with The Grey Wolf and still stay afloat. It would only be six months. Six months with the man I'd craved since we were younger.

He'd said he'd make it so my family took me back, and I believed him. Not sure why, but it was there. Yes, that fear still rode me, but with Luca, he seemed to make it all melt away.

Doing this would help, and I wouldn't have to worry about my pack financially. That was the goal. The rest ... I'd deal with it when my six months were up.

"There will be no other women in your bed, Luca. I'm serious. One and the deal's off and you pay the money, even though I leave. It's my only stipulation." Being in his bed was a strange concept, but having another wolf in there wouldn't work for me. I'd always been a very monogamous woman, not jumping from bed to bed. I'd only had a few boyfriends, but none lasted long. While I was with them, though, there was no other.

Luca's reputation was that of a bed hopper. No way I'd subject myself to that while living under the same roof as him.

He nodded. "That, I concede to."

"I can't believe you're doing this."

He cupped the side of my face, and a small sigh left my mouth. "Believe it, my beautiful Caleigh. I'll make everything you want come true."

My heart warmed and something deep inside me settled. This was going to change my life forever.

CHAPTER FOUR

THE WALK INTO MY HOME WAS FILLED WITH A MIX OF dread and excitement, which was a strange combination. There was almost an eeriness of what I was about to do clouding around me. It was what was best for my family and reminding myself of that helped some.

"What's up?" Ren called from the couch of the family room as I entered, shutting the door behind me. Eyes came to me, along with smiles from my pack. A rock hit my gut at the thought of not seeing them every day. Not eating meals at the family table. Not having my brothers give me shit on a normal basis.

"What's Sage got goin' on?" my other brother, Marcus, called from the kitchen. He wouldn't admit it, but he'd had his eye on my best friend for years. She, too, hadn't gone through her heat cycle; therefore, my brother had stayed away.

A female wolf's heat cycle was the beginning of finding a mate. During that time, our bodies changed and our scent emanated from our pours, calling to our mate. Most female wolves found their mate within a year of going through the cycle. Personally, I felt my brother stayed away from Sage because he didn't want any fall out when it came to her and I. Why? I had no clue.

"I need you, Ren, Stu, Mom, and Dad to meet me in Dad's office please."

Ren leapt off the couch, and Stu came to me from the kitchen, both their eyes holding concern. Inside, I felt nervous, so I had no idea what I looked like on the outside. Whatever it was sent my brothers in state of alarm, which wasn't what I had wanted.

"Are you alright?" Marcus asked, brushing his hand against my arm reassuringly. His nose went up in the air as he sniffed. When his eyes pinched together, I knew he smelled Luca on me. Our sense of smell was very acute. I had already figured having him all over me would help my cause.

"I'm good." I plastered on a smile, thinking about Luca and what it would be like to have his touch on me. The smile turned genuine, which was what I was going for. "We just need to talk. I have some exciting news."

Ren's eyes narrowed on me. He and I had always been closer than myself and my other brothers. If anyone, this would be harder for him to take, but I had to make it work. This bargain was for the best and would help my pack. I'd already committed to it, so there was no backing out.

"Come on; I'll go get Dad and Stu." Marcus took off down the hallway while the other wolves in the room looked at me speculatively. Instead of saying anything to them, I followed Ren to our father's office.

Not two minutes later, my father, mother, Marcus, and Stu entered the room, their noses instantly flaring.

Before anyone could say anything, I blurted, "I found my mate!"

The air in the room turned. While all my brothers had some alpha in them, Marcus and Stu weren't considered alphas, but with the vibes everyone was giving off, that could be argued.

"No," my father answered, even though I hadn't asked a question, more like made a statement.

My mother gasped, placing her hand over her mouth and not hiding the shock in her eyes.

Not being in the heat cycle, I had known how this would be and smoothing it over would be difficult. Nevertheless, I could do it.

"Yeah, Dad. You'll be very excited!"

"I highly doubt that," he responded, running his hand through his hair.

"Who?" Ren asked, crossing his arms over his chest, still giving off alpha waves that threatened to knock me on my ass.

"Luca."

My mother moved forward, placing her hands on my arms and looking deeply into my eyes. "This can't be, Caleigh."

Giving my mother a bright smile, I said, "Yes, it is. We just discovered it today. I'm gathering my things and moving in with him."

"What?" Ren came up and brushed my hair away from my neck. "He hasn't marked you."

Shit, I hadn't thought about that. I had to think quickly on my toes.

"We're saving that until after I tell you. He wanted to show my pack respect. He's also coming to pick me up in an hour."

"Darling girl, you haven't gone through heat. How can

you know he's your mate?" my father asked as my brothers looked at me with expressions of bafflement.

I gave a shrug, making all this up as I went along. Damn, this sucked.

"Mom, you've told me yourself that the heat cycle isn't a sure-fire way to tell one's mate. You said that, back in the day, females could detect their mate before the cycle hit. Then, once it did, it was confirmed." Light flashed in her eyes, and I had no doubt she was regretting sharing that small piece of information with me. "I've found mine."

"What if you're wrong?"

That was the million-dollar question, because I was wrong. I'd be done with this in six months and needed to find a safe haven. I'd need to come back to my family.

I pushed back all my fears and gave it to them honestly. "If I'm wrong, then I pray to the heavens that I still have a home here with you."

"My girl, you always have a home here," my father started, warming my heart and alleviating some of the fear I felt about being a lone wolf. "I just don't think you should jump into this without knowing for sure. Luca ... well, he's a good man, but he's ..."

"Screwed everything in the area, plus some," Marcus added, obviously not liking the fact that his little sister was going with a man with a reputation like Luca's. I didn't really like that part of it, either, but wolves were sexual creatures and the alphas were especially.

I turned toward my brother. "I know this. Things have changed, and those times are over."

"Why now?" Ren questioned. "What happened that made you decide this?"

"I was at his place with Sage and it just clicked. We talked and that was it. Please just trust me."

"You're doing this of your own free will?" my mother asked straight out. It's what I loved about her the most. She was honest and to the point, not messing around with other details.

Giving her a wide smile, I told her, "Yes. Totally of my free will."

She turned toward my father. "Then we need to respect it."

"I don't like it," my father responded.

"Didn't say you did." My mother turned back to me after giving a look to my brothers. "If this is what you want, then we'll stand beside you. What about work?"

While my moment of happiness came at them believing me, it fled when the discussion of work came up. I hadn't talked to Luca about that, but no way I'd leave my family in the lurch.

"I'm still working."

"Not sure how that's gonna work, darlin' girl," my father responded. The truth was, I didn't either, considering I'd be with another pack and knowing the ins and out of my home pack weren't conducive to pack life. That would be something I'd have to talk to Luca about.

"It'll work out, Dad. Now I have to go pack. I'm only going to take a few things with me. I'll be back in a couple of days for the rest. Is that okay?"

My mother tightly wrapped her arms around me. "I'm going to miss you, baby girl."

Tears sprang to my eyes. It took everything I had to push them back. My mother had been my rock since I was born, and not having that formed an ache in my heart so strong it felt like it could knock me down.

"I will."

My three brothers gave me hugs, not happy one bit

about it, but knowing I had my own free will, so there wasn't anything they could do. My father hugged me and started to tear up. This big strong man was utterly sad I was leaving and that shoved a knife in me and twisted. *This is for you, Daddy.*

Rushing from the room, I packed several bags with clothes, toiletries, pictures, and keepsakes. While I knew I'd be back, I tried to grab as much as possible, knowing that if I were really going with my mate, I'd take everything I could. If I didn't, my family would become suspicious of my actions.

"Caleigh, Luca's here!" Marcus's voice came from the bottom of the stairs, bellowing up. This was it.

Looking around my room, I looked at the pictures of my family lining the walls, along with a beach landscape that I loved so much. My bedspread was a deep purple that laid on top of my queen-sized bed, which I didn't pack up because I didn't think I'd need it.

I'd lived in this room my entire life. These four walls held so many thoughts and secrets. So much laughter, hopes, and dreams. So many dirty thoughts of a certain man who was downstairs now, waiting to take me to his home. I could do this.

Picking up one of the bags, I hauled it down the stairs. My brothers, mother, and father all met me at the bottom, while the pack was around in the living room, all watching with avid eyes.

Luca stood by the front door, a sexy smile on his lips and a gleam in his eye. Knowing I needed to make a statement, I dropped my bag, rushed into his arms and wrapped mine around him. His came around me and squeezed me firmly, and then he placed a kiss on the top of my head.

"My beautiful Caleigh," he said softly, and my body

relaxed into him like it had done it thousands of times before.

"Son," my father called out.

I didn't move from Luca's arms, but I did turn my head so I could see my father.

"Yes, sir," Luca said respectfully, giving me a comforting squeeze. I knew he liked my father because of all the business they did together and our history. With Luca being a powerful alpha, it said a lot for him to address him this way, and I liked it.

"Normally, I'd never ask this, but given this situation, I feel I must." Luca's body didn't move as he listened to my father. "Don't you feel that you should wait until her heat? There's a chance she's not your mate, and you don't want to put my daughter through that realization."

Luca didn't budge, yet strong waves came off him, permeating the air and suffocating the oxygen from the room. "All due respect, she's my mate. She's coming to me of her own free will, and I do not appreciate you thinking anything but."

My father didn't succumb to the pulses in the air. "I get that; understand it. What I'm saying is: why not wait until you're sure? I don't want my daughter hurt."

A low growl came from Luca. "I'd never hurt Caleigh." I felt it and squeezed tighter, hoping to calm the beast inside that was threatening to escape. How I felt this, I didn't know, but it was there, powerful and fierce.

Luca's nose came to my hair, and he inhaled. I felt his body lose a bit of the starch, but not much. When his breathing returned to calm, I knew he was better. This wouldn't work out if he lost his cool with my family.

"Dad, we're leaving," I announced, breaking up the tête-à-tête between the two most powerful alphas I knew. No way I'd want there to be a fight between them. "I appreciate your concern, but this is going to be great."

"Do you have more bags?" Luca asked.

"Yes, in my room."

"I'll get them," Ren said, sulking up the stairs and coming back down moments later.

I gave hugs to my family as Luca led me out of the house and to his car.

"What about my car?" I asked, looking up at him.

"Give me the keys, and one of the pack members will get it tomorrow."

I nodded as Ren went to the back of the truck and tossed my bags inside. Luca had a huge, black four-by-four that lifted off the ground pretty high. I'd have to hoist my ass up there to get in.

Ren stepped up to me, and I heard a growl from Luca. He was taking this mate thing very seriously, giving all the actions a real mate would give his female.

Ren wrapped his arms around me, holding me close. "Cal, you come home at any time. Our door is always open. Do not think for one second you have to stay with Luca and his pack. Your home is here—don't ever forget that."

My heart constricted.

"She will be with me," Luca ordered as Ren snapped his neck up at the tone. "Caleigh is mine." The fierceness in the words made me tremble, and Ren felt it.

"You sure this is of your own free will?" he questioned, and then Luca was right there, pulling me out of Ren's arms.

"Brother or not, this will not end well if you keep it up," Luca warned.

Luca and Ren went into a stare down, and I had to jump in.

"Ren. I promise you, this is of my own free will. I wouldn't do something I didn't want to. You know that."

Ren leaned down and placed a kiss on my cheek, which made Luca growl again.

"Come, let's get you home." Luca led me to the truck and helped me inside, then slammed the door. He rounded the front, jumped in, and then backed out.

I gave Ren a soft wave as we left the only home I'd ever known and I entered into my new life. No matter how temporary it was.

CHAPTER FIVE

LUCA DROVE STRAIGHT TO HIS HOME, HOLDING MY hand the entire time. It felt comforting to know he was thinking about me and wanted me to feel safe. I'd always felt safe around him, even when I was younger. Now this was a whole different level that I was trying to piece together.

"I feel your nerves coming off you. There's no need for it. My pack will accept you."

"Do they know about our deal?" I didn't know how I'd feel about the answer either way, but I felt the need to ask.

"No, beautiful. Not even Sage. But she's smart. I have no doubt she'll put the pieces together. I'll speak with her."

I rested my head on the back of the seat. "I don't understand why you want to do this. Why tie yourself to me for six months?"

He lifted my hand to his lips, kissing it softly. His beard tickled my hand. "My sweet Caleigh. In the next six months, I will show you."

"Show me what?"

"How beautiful our life will be together."

My hand jolted. "You mean for six months."

He smiled. "Yes, of course."

Everything he said seemed to be in code, one I couldn't understand, but would damn well figure out. It wasn't like I didn't have time. I'd always loved a good puzzle, even as a kid. This only sparked my interest.

Pulling up to Luca's home, it was like all the other times I'd been here. Nothing had changed appearance-wise, yet inside, something had. This was going to be my home for the next six months, and I needed to treat it as such, meaning standing my ground on many things.

Wolves were very territorial, especially female wolves. Having a new wolf come in was going to be an adjustment. I'd seen it many times in my pack when one of the males would take on a female. My mother, the alpha female of the pack, would have to stand her ground and not allow the newbie to come in and think she would take her place in the hierarchy.

That had happened several times. I'd seen my mother in several fights because of it, ones I couldn't participate in because it would show my mother had a weakness and that was something she didn't have.

My plan wasn't to start fighting with all the females, but I needed to show my place, and if a situation came up, I'd need to be prepared to handle it. This could go either good or bad. That was up to the future. One thing I knew for certain was I would have my head held high, shoulders back and to attention when I walked into the home this time. I wouldn't allow myself to feel small or weak in any way, no matter what was thrown at me.

Luca had said his pack would accept me, but that didn't mean they all would. Especially the already pronounced alpha female, Natalie, who Sage had told me was a royal bitch.

My eyes were wide open. I knew I'd have to be on my game.

Fighting was nothing new. My brothers had taught me everything I knew and then some. Watching them in battle, I'd picked up my own unique techniques. Whereas they'd fought to the death several times—each one I had hated more than the next—I had not. Being the daughter of the alpha female, most people left me alone. In Luca's pack, I didn't think I'd fair as lucky, even if I didn't want to have to fight.

It didn't mean I wouldn't.

"Caleigh, tell me what's on your mind," Luca said in his deep voice, reaching over after throwing the truck in park and unlatching my seatbelt. "Something is bothering you."

"This whole situation is bothering me, Luca. How am I supposed to pretend I'm your mate for six months? You know I won't be able to let comments or other wolves slide if they give me trouble. Are you okay with me possibly fighting with your pack to secure my position only to leave in six months and have them all wondering what the hell is going on?"

He turned, placed his hand under my chin, and directed me to give him my eyes, which I did. "You do what you have to. This is your pack. You are my mate. Everything else, we take in stride."

"You know Natalie is going to be a problem."

Luca gave a reassuring smile. "I have no doubt you can hold your own with her. Just live this with me. Live these six months as my mate one hundred percent. You and me. Can you do that for me?"

"Live it real? How real?"

A sexy smirk played on his lips, making my thighs quiver. "Every step real. Every touch. Every action. Every thought. Every kiss. Every moment for six months, absolutely no holding back ... anything."

My breath caught in my throat as all the thoughts of our relationship being real swirled in my head like a tornado. Wolves were very physical and emotional beings. Touches would be often. Kisses even more so. All of those would reel into the emotional, putting my heart on the line for something that wouldn't last.

It was rare for wolves to mate without having the scent that attracted each other. The chances of us having that were slim to none. That would mean in six months' time, my heart would shatter and bend. Like everything else in my life, though, I'd pick the pieces up and move on. I had to remember this was for my family—the reasoning for all this.

Once I found my true mate, he would heal all the wounds I knew would form. The time between would be the hardest, though.

"Yes, I can do that."

Luca pulled me to him and placed a soft kiss on my lips. "That's my beautiful girl. Let's go meet your pack."

I shook my head, for once feeling nervous about entering this house. It only lasted a moment, because showing the pack fear would never be an option.

Sucking in a breath, I opened the truck door. Luca, being super-fast, came to my side and helped me down. The front of my body brushed against his toned one, and I inhaled his scent, one I'd memorized many years ago, but this was different. This time, Luca was mine.

The front door swung open and Jonas, Luca's brother and beta, stood there, eyes alert and posture stiff.

"Jonas, get some of the guys to get Caleigh's things from

the back of my truck. Take them to my room then meet me in my office in fifteen," Luca said as we walked up to the house, his arm slung over my shoulders as he pulled me tightly against his body.

"Caleigh?" My name came out more as a question than a comment, as if he couldn't believe it was me that his brother and alpha had his arm draped over, guiding me into the house. "Alpha?"

"Fifteen in my office. You and Niko. Send Sage in, in thirty."

Jonas cleared his throat. "Of course." He turned his smile to me. "Hey there, little one; how are ya?"

Some of the weight left my shoulders at his words, but Luca didn't think it so. Instead, he growled.

"Don't. She's mine. Got it?"

Shock crossed Jonas's features, but he masked them quickly. "Of course, Alpha." He leaned into the house and whistled for someone. Seconds later, two guys came out, their eyes doing the same as Jonas's.

"Truck. Everything inside goes to Alpha's room."

The two men paused, looking between their alpha and I.

"Now!" Jonas barked, snapping the two out of their thoughts as they left and made their way to the truck.

Luca pulled me in through the doors and directly to his office, all the while I noticed questionable stares from the other wolves. All I could do was smile softly to them and follow as Luca pulled me along.

He shut the door to his office and pulled me into his arms, looking down at me with fire in his eyes. A fire that reminded me of the campfires we used to have as kids when we'd sit by each other, but not too close, and he'd talk to his friends while I was with Sage. We were together, yet not. Strange how that memory just came up.

"Do you want to kiss me?"

My lips parted because, yes, yes, I did want to kiss him.

Giving a slight nod, he stared me down. "Then you kiss me without hesitation. Any time you want. Wherever we are. There is no questioning it. There is no second-guessing. You feel it, you do it."

"So, if I want to slap you because you're being an asshole?"

Luca gave off the sexiest chuckle, his arms getting securely around me. "Just be prepared for me to stop you."

My eyes narrowed, but I really didn't feel the slightest bit pissed. I just liked the teasing aspect we were going for here. It made me feel good, so I kept the ball rolling.

"I'd like to see you try."

Luca threw back his head and laughed, a sound I hadn't heard since we were kids, except this was deeper and more meaningful.

Everything inside of me warmed. I wanted to kiss him.

As soon as he brought his head back, I stood on my tiptoes and laid a powerful and deep kiss on him. His laughter died as he kissed me back, threading his hand through my hair and twisting forcefully. The bite of pain turned me on, and my core clenched forcefully.

I pressed my body firmly against his, feeling the hardness of his cock against my waist. My wolf growled and snarled, wanting more than I was giving her, but I couldn't stop myself. His taste, feel, and smell were invading my senses, taking over in a way that was turning into a craving, one I couldn't get enough of.

A loud knock came to the door, and I jumped, pulling

away from Luca, who growled, his eyes narrowing on the door.

"You told them to come," I whispered, reminding him.

"That doesn't mean I have to like getting interrupted." He brushed his lips over mine then called out, "In."

Jonas and Niko strode inside, first taking in our closeness, then inhaling the scents in the room. My arousal was there on full display, for them all. There was no hiding it.

"Alpha," they both greeted, then, "Caleigh."

"Hi," I called out softly to the men, giving a flick of my hand, to which Luca pulled me forcefully to him. He had this "real" thing down pat already.

"Caleigh is my mate."

The dumbfounded looks on the men's faces was priceless. If I weren't in the situation I was in, I would have laughed.

"I'll announce it to the pack tonight."

Niko looked around to my neck. "She's not marked."

"And she won't be until I decide it's time."

"What's going on here?" Jonas questioned, and I felt my blood pressure rise.

Luca didn't miss a beat. "Caleigh and I have known each other since we were pups. We are mates, and nothing else needs to be said about it."

Jonas rubbed his hand over his face. "Alpha, are you sure about this?"

Sadly, I took that as a direct hit to my self-esteem. It almost sounded like he was disappointed Luca had chosen me to be his mate. I'd never had any problems with Jonas during my times here, but I'd never been in the fold, either. There were many circumstances surrounding this bargain, and I had a feeling it would be blown on the first day.

Alpha waves filled the room. "You dare disobey?"

Jonas lowered his head. "Of course not, Alpha. I just want what's right for you."

"Caleigh is what's right. End of discussion. Leave."

They both gave me a look then sauntered out the door.

"Well, that went well," I murmured, pulling out of Luca's arms and giving us a bit of distance. "This is how it's going to be for everyone. They aren't going to believe we're mates."

"I should mark you." He said those four words like they were causal and not something that would totally entangle my world into his forever.

If he bit me, there would be no going back. At least, not on his end. On my end, if I didn't mark him, we could still break, but it would be more difficult for him to sever that link. We'd be partially bonded in a way that would be painful to sever. It wasn't impossible, but it's so rare that I didn't know if this would be good for us.

Not only that, would it impact me finding my true mate later after this deal was over? Then why did it feel so right at the same time? That thought scared me the most, because it shouldn't feel right.

"We need to think about that. *You* need to think about that."

He stepped closer, confidence radiating from him. "I'd mark you right now and not look back."

The world around me fell away, leaving only him and I in the middle of an empty space. We gazed deeply into each other's eyes. I wasn't sure what I was searching for. Whatever it was, it was powerful. It was something that struck me deep from within. This strong alpha wanted so badly to tie himself to me that he would mark me and take on that pain when the six months was up.

A knock on the door and a swoosh of it opening put all

the pieces of the world back together again, breaking our moment as Sage walked in.

"Care to tell me what's going on?" She didn't address her brother. She addressed me.

"We're mates," I announced, like it's the most normal thing in the world. Hell, one day around Luca and I was already doing his thing.

"What!" she screeched, her eyes darting back and forth between her brother and myself.

"Calm down, Sage," Luca ordered.

Her assessing eyes went to him. "Calm down? I tell you what's going on in her life and now you're mated? What's up with that, Luca? Are you blackmailing her?" Her nose twisted up in disgust.

"Watch how you speak to me, Sage," Luca warned from deep in his throat. "What Caleigh and I have is between us. You are not to say a word to anyone about what you know. It stays between the three of us, and that is all."

"Are you going to tell me what this is?" she charged, putting her hands on her hips and angling out her foot. From many years of being friends with her, I knew this was a position of don't fuck with me and she would get answers.

Luca wasn't having it.

"Yes. That's all you need to know."

"You haven't marked her. No one here is going to believe she's your mate if she's not marked. Let alone, we can't smell it."

I'd forgotten about that—the smell of mated pairs. Once the pair marked each other, their scents became mingled and entwined with one another, creating their own unique scent. The only way to start this process was the marking. *Crap.*

"You let me deal with that," Luca announced, pulling me close to his body.

"Are you okay?" Sage asked me, and Luca's body went taut at the accusation. I reached out and rubbed his hand to try to calm him.

"Yes, perfectly."

"Go."

Sage looked at her brother. "You'd better not be screwing over my friend." She didn't give Luca a chance to respond before she marched out the door, slamming it in her wake.

"This is just going smashing, Luca."

He brushed the hair away from my ear. "It will be perfect."

My insides shivered and quivered.

"Now, let's show you to your room—our room."

Heavens, help me.

CHAPTER SIX

"THE MONEY IS ALREADY IN YOUR FATHER'S ACCOUNT under Ivan's name. It was done before I picked you up; therefore, no one would draw a connection."

I breathed out a deep breath, thankful my family was now out of debt and would be able to get back on track. All of this would be worth it to get my family back on their feet so they didn't have to worry.

"I tossed in another fifty grand to help."

"What?"

As we entered his bedroom, he pulled me into his arms, slamming the door behind us. "That was free." Then he kissed me, long, wet, and deeply. After several moments, he pulled away, leaving me a bit off balance, unable to ask him about the extra money.

"Welcome to your new home." He held his arm out, and my gaze followed, taking in the expanse of the room. My hand flew to my neck. I swore there was no oxygen in the space.

It was incredible.

Three of the walls were painted a light blue, but as my

gaze traveled the length, it somehow turned into a grayish color. It was like some kind of magic, how the color changed depending on the lighting in the room.

A very large landscape print hung on one of the walls. It was absolutely breathtaking, with its open fields that turned into meadows, with its vast amounts of trees and a waterfall that splashed down to a pond where fish swam.

The fourth wall was covered in stone from top to bottom with a fireplace placed center. A large television hung above, but it was the stonework that was gorgeous. Someone had to have laid each of those stones by hand.

In the center of one of the bluish/grayish walls was a huge bed. It was so large it had to have been custom-made. I'd never seen a mattress that large. It was dressed in a large, dark gray bedspread with lots of pillows at the top. Masculine, yet not so much so a female wouldn't feel welcome. It's perfect.

What stood out with the bed were the four mahogany posts that looked as if they could reach the ceiling. I stepped closer to investigate and noted carvings, hundreds of them throughout the wood. Wolves in all different shapes, sizes, and positions, along with trees of forests throughout.

"This is breathtaking," I whispered, running my hand over the wood and feeling several of the grooves.

"This bed has been passed down through the generations of my pack. Every alpha since the pack began has slept in this bed at some point when they were alpha."

"This is just beyond words, Luca."

Two large dressers were against a wall, along with two nightstands on either side of the bed. Next to the fireplace were two comfy looking chairs and a coffee table. The room was simple, yet everything went together so meticulously.

Luca moved his hands up my arms, and my heart quickened as he dipped his head to my ear. "You're perfect," he whispered, making my core clench as the heat level in the room began to rise.

He brushed his lips against my neck then moved down my shoulder, darting his tongue out and licking from my shirt all the way up to my ear. He then grazed the same path with his teeth, his beard adding to the sensations and my knees went weak.

"Think about my mark. Here." He grazed again. "For everyone to see. For everyone to know that you're mine and I'm yours. That I'm the only male on this earth who will touch you, taste you, and make you come."

My body full-out shivered as Luca wrapped his arm around my waist and pulled me snugly to his taut body. The steel length of him pressed against my back, showing me exactly how aroused he was.

"Like that idea? Want everyone to know that I claim you. That I fuck you and only you?"

A whimper escaped as I brutally clutched the arm around me, digging my nails in.

It was true, I did. Not only that, his words were such a turn on that I felt a strong possibility I could come just from them.

"Let me tell you what I'm going to do." He nipped the lobe of my ear, not hard, but it did leave a bite of pain that made me jump a bit. "I'm going to use my claws to tear the clothes away from your creamy skin. I'll trace my index claw down your neck, between your breasts, and to your navel, not cutting, but bringing the heat of your body and arousal to the surface."

My hips jumped.

"I'll lay you on the bed and kiss every inch of your skin, working my way down to that soft spot between your legs."

Not being able to take any more of his talking, I turned in his arms, planted my lips on his, and rubbed my body up and down his. I laced my fingers through his hair, pulling him forcefully to my body as he kissed me back fiercely and deeply.

Everything electrified as he ripped my shirt over my head, then used his claws to cut my bra. It was hot, so fucking hot.

I tore his shirt from him then stopped to enjoy the view. He was muscled perfection. Broad shoulders that tapered down his chest to his taut abs and down to the sexy as hell V that disappeared under his jeans. As wetness pooled below, I shifted on my feet, hoping to get a little friction down there.

Luca wasted no time removing his jeans and underwear, standing in front of me in all his beautiful perfection. His cock was long and thick, with veins throbbing, and a head that looked an angry purple and ready to burst.

He pulled me to him, kissing me deeply as he removed my pants. I kicked them off, helping, and then spread my legs wide. My wolf inside was completely on board with everything that was about to happen.

"I'm going to fuck you, Caleigh."

"Heavens, yes," I groaned out as he roamed my body, leaving heat every place his hands touched.

"I want to mark you."

It took a few minutes for my brain to catch up.

"Luca, that's a huge step. Are you prepared for the consequences?"

His sexy smile came out as he looked me square in my eyes. "I'm prepared for it all."

I couldn't breathe. The arousal was so high as he

pushed me into the bed with his weight, adding extra pressure on me.

I wanted it. Wanted his mark on me. Wanted to be his. I'd wanted it for as long as I could remember, and now it was coming true. Even if it were for a short period of time, I was going to take it. *Live it real.*

"Yes," I whispered.

His eyes flashed from the brown with golden rims to full-out gold. I could see his wolf staring back at me hungrily. He wanted this, too.

He kissed me vigorously and wetly. Then I felt the tip of his cock at my entrance as he shifted his hips. Luca slid inside me inch by inch, never once letting go of my lips, his hands on either side of my head, holding me in place. It was so damn intimate that tears sprang to my eyes and I had to push them back.

He seated himself inside me completely then stopped, only pulling away to look deeply into my eyes, seeing everything I had for him. It was scary, but there was no way to hide it. The moment was life-altering. There was no coming back from it.

"You're so fucking beautiful. Always have been."

At those words, Luca didn't hold back. His thrusts pushed me so far up the bed my head threatened to hit the headboard and he had to pull me back down. Each delicious stroke of him inside me scraped me in so many ways that I was already close to coming. So very, very close.

He pulled out and pushed in fast and fiercely. His sexy as hell noises came from deep in his throat, and I couldn't hide my grunts and moans.

I was on the cusp, right there, as his pelvis bone hit my clit repeatedly.

"I'm gonna come," I gasped.

Luca's eyes flashed wolf. He picked up speed, bringing his mouth down as I arched my back. Then he bit me.

As soon as his teeth went into my flesh, I brutally screamed out my climax, my entire body shaking uncontrollably. The bite only intensified an already combustible orgasm, taking me to an entirely different level, one I didn't know if I'd survive from.

Luca pulled his teeth away, licking the bite, and only then did my body relax and fall to the bed, the tension falling out of it. I sucked in breath as my heart hammered inside my chest like I was on some kind of drug.

That's when I felt it. A change inside of me. It started at my neck where he bit. Then, like a spider web, it grew, adding links everywhere it could until my entire insides were covered in webs.

"The bond," I whispered, looking up at Luca who had a strange look on his face. I wondered if I had the same reaction on mine.

It was happening to him—the connection between us—and it was wrong.

"It's not supposed to happen to me until I bite you."

Only then did he come back and focus on me.

"You have it, too?"

"Yes. I'm scared." And I was. The bond was nothing to mess around with. He said he could hack it, but I didn't know if I could. Not with the feelings I'd had for Luca all my life.

He rolled off to my side, pulling me tightly to his body, somehow still connected to him. This made it more intimate.

"I know you are, but beautiful, you have nothing to fear. I swear it."

"How can you be so sure?" He was so damn confident

and riding this wave like he'd wanted this. Wanted me to feel what he was feeling. "What happens when I go into heat? My wolf wanted this, but what if she decides you aren't my mate. What happens then? This will kill us."

"Let's worry about that when the time comes. Right now, live this with me," he repeated the words from earlier.

I let out a deep breath, beginning to feel his heartbeat inside of me. The bond was growing quickly. So much faster than the stories I'd heard about mates connecting.

"Don't hurt me." The vulnerability in my voice made me want to kick myself for opening my lips, but they were out there.

"Never." His words came out soft, and when he kissed me, it was sweet, kind, and caring. A kiss that seared deep inside my soul, attaching itself to me like nothing I'd ever experienced.

It was the beginning. The beginning of the end.

CHAPTER SEVEN

As we entered the dining area, hand in hand, a hush fell over the room.

The space was large, fitting several tables with bench seats, some had chairs. The tables looked old and possibly handmade. The walls were a bright cream with large, thick wooden planks along the top for a decorative, cabin-type feel. There were large beams that spanned from one end to the other, adding to the appeal.

I felt the eyes. All of them, and there were thirty, maybe thirty-five or so, pairs on us. The nervousness I thought I'd feel didn't come. Instead, confidence filled me, and I felt my spine straightening. My wolf felt it, too, as she snarled inside, ready to fight if need be. I was, too. Luca had told me to live this with him, and that meant fully. I wasn't going to back down.

"Hello." I gave a soft wave with the hand Luca didn't have ahold of, while he squeezed the other.

"I'd like everyone to welcome Caleigh to the pack ... my mate."

Shocked looks came from the peanut gallery, along with

gasps from some of the female wolves.

I searched for Natalie, but she wasn't in attendance. Pity. I would have liked to set all of this to rest now.

"That's just not possible." A female I knew as Gabby said. I also knew she was close friends with Natalie, according to Sage.

"He bit her," Jonas, the beta, said from his seat. "It's as possible as it gets."

I noted Sage sitting at one of the tables, her hand resting on her neck in the exact spot the mark Luca had given me was on my body. Her eyes were concerned, and I felt the urge to go over to her and reassure her, but the truth was, I didn't know what to say.

"Well, she's no alpha. You gonna have two bitches in your bed?" George, an older wolf, said from a side table. "Heaven knows we need a strong alpha bitch to lead this pack. She ain't it." His judgement of me cut to the quick.

Inside, my wolf growled, snarled, and clawed at me to get out. What George didn't know was that I was in fact an alpha wolf. In my family, I had just never acted on it. There'd been no need, considering my father and brothers ran the pack and I hadn't gone into heat yet. Therefore, showing that alpha would only draw more losers into my life than I needed.

Luca began to speak, but I squeezed his hand hard, getting his attention. If he wanted me to live this with him, then he needed to respect me, and that I knew how to handle these situations.

He shut up.

I hadn't let my waves off before, so I didn't know if it would work, but I gave it a try while looking the man square in the eyes.

"No one will be in Luca's bed but me. I'm the only bitch

he needs. The only bitch this pack needs. Remember that."

He smiled. "Well, this should be interesting." He clasped his hands behind his head and leaned back.

Luca pulled me to his side, kissed the top of my head, then declared, "Let's eat."

I WOKE up in Luca's arms, the same place I'd been over the past several days. He hadn't let me up except to go to the bathroom and eat, saying we needed to consummate our mating. When I'd said our *non-existent mating*, he hadn't taken that too well, fucking me until I'd felt that connection burn so hot I swore it would melt my insides.

He'd been right, though. That bond inside of me was latching on like tree roots, imbedding deeply. Each moment only scared me as to what our future held. The temptation to bite him was riding me hard with each passing moment.

Without a word, Luca rolled me onto my back, kissing a trail down my naked body then latching on to my pussy. I threaded my fingers through his hair, holding him to me, grinding my hips against his mouth and getting as much friction as I could. Luca was magnificent with this lips, tongue, and teeth down there. He knew exactly what he was doing.

Heat built inside me, and my orgasm was right there, hanging off a cliff. He must have sensed it because he removed his mouth, climbed on top of me, and then slammed his hard cock inside of me while lacing our fingers together by the side of my head.

"Fucking love your pussy." He thrusted deeply, rattling the bed. "You're fucking perfect."

I groaned, arching my back and thrusting my breasts up.

His hips became like pistons, firing at a rapid rate. I dug my nails into his shoulders and screamed as the climax hit. Luca bit me, causing another wave of explosions to crash over me like a tidal wave taking me out to sea.

He had a thing. Every time he made me come, he bit me. Sometimes in the same spot. Other times in different places. I said nothing. I liked it, and so did my wolf. She howled each time he sunk his teeth in me.

Luca groaned out his release, licking my wound and sealing up the blood flow. We weren't vampires or anything like that, but we did have a special something in our saliva that stopped the flow of blood. He'd used it … a lot.

He rolled over, pulling out of me and flopping onto the bed. I curled into him, resting my head on his chest and listening to his rapid breathing.

I loved that I did this to him—turned him on so much that his orgasms knocked the air right from his lungs. It gave me a sense of power that this strong alpha was completely wiped and out of breath because of what we'd just done. That was hot.

"I got work to do today," Luca said, looking deeply into my eyes. "Don't want to, but I can't stay in bed all the time, fucking your brains out."

"That was your decision, captain," I teased.

He brought his arms around me, holding me securely. "Yeah, it was. We needed that time."

The time he talked about was what scared me. Without me biting him, the connection between us was relentlessly pulling at me. A true test of how powerful it was would be for us to separate for a while—him doing his thing for a while and me mine. Then we could see if that connection was still strong. Most mates didn't like to be away from each other for long periods of time.

I remembered a time when my father had gone away on business and left my mother home with me and my brothers. We'd been young, and my mother hadn't wanted to leave us. She'd been in agony at one point, physically hurting because her mate was nowhere around.

This was what I feared.

If Luca and I parted and we had this reaction, it would end up killing us both. This was not the bargain we had set up, but there's no going back.

"I need to go to Howls; see if they need help and what my hours are."

"My wolf isn't going to like other shifters around you, Caleigh. Are you sure you want to keep working there?"

I shifted my hand to cup his face. "Until everything gets back up and running, I have to help."

He sighed deeply. "Right. Let's get you up and dressed." Luca kissed me, rolled off, and then pulled me to my feet. "First, shower." He pulled me with him, and we had a magnificent shower.

"WELL, look who decided to grace us with their presence," Niko said with a wide smile on his face as he sat at the kitchen counter, holding a chip between his fingers.

"He finally let me out," I joked back, sliding onto the stool a couple down from him, Luca sitting right next to me.

"Looks like he used you as a chew toy." This came from Jonas, who moseyed on into the room.

"Damn right." Luca smiled, thoroughly proud of what he had done.

"I'm lucky I still have blood."

The men around me chuckled.

I moved to get up. "I need food."

Luca placed his hand on my thigh. "I'll get what you need."

"It's seriously hot that you want to, but no, you won't."

His brow rose in question.

"I'm not one of those women who wants to be waited on hand and foot. I'm completely capable of doing many things on my own, including feeding myself."

"I like her," Jonas said.

I smiled full-out, getting up from my spot and making myself a sandwich. I even asked Luca if he wanted one and made one for him, as well. I'd never been a woman who wanted to be waited on. I wasn't overly pretentious with makeup and hair, either, but I always tried to look nice.

While we ate and chatted, I had to wonder where everyone was, because this was a big pack. Regardless, I liked not having too many around and being able to adjust.

We'd just finished eating when I heard, "Look what the garbage tossed back." Natalie entered the room, her long blonde hair waving behind her as she strutted in. There was no other word for it. It was a strut.

"Here we go," Niko said, but I ignored him.

"Hi, Natalie. Nice to see you," I lied.

She rolled her eyes as she strode up to the side of the counter facing directly in front of me. "I'm alpha bitch around here, and you'd better learn it. Don't step on my toes, or I'll dismantle you," she warned.

I felt the smile lines come to my eyes as my lips tipped up. "Aw, that's such a great hello."

"I don't give a shit." I felt her waves hit me, and I gave off some of my own, repelling hers. It was a test of wills, and I had nothing but time.

Her eyes narrowed, and then she threw out more, but it wasn't enough.

She was the first to shake her head. Surprisingly, she didn't challenge me, which I would have thought would be the first thing she did.

She looked to Niko. "Make me a sandwich," she ordered.

Niko looked at me and rolled his eyes. "Make your own damn food."

She placed her hand on her hip and jetted out her foot, just like Sage did when she was pissed off. "This is how you allow the men to treat the women in your pack, Luca?"

"Maybe you should get off your ass and make your own," I responded. "Only lazy bitches need men to do things for them. Once in a while, great. But everyday shit when you're more than capable, no."

She charged toward me, pointing her finger in my face. "You fucking bitch," she spat.

I wanted to laugh.

"That's the best you got? You need to work on that, honey."

"You're—"

"Incoming!" was yelled from the doorway, and Luca jumped up from his seat. Natalie halted her words as the guys followed Luca.

"Talk to me," Luca ordered.

"Six wolves, unknown, on the back edge and coming this way rapid fire."

"Fuck," Luca said. "Caleigh, you stay here. The rest of you, out."

"Oh no!" I charged forward. "I'm not sitting back on my hands, waiting. Let's do this."

"Our wolves don't know you well yet. I don't want

anything to happen to you."

"Oh, that's it; coddle her," Natalie chimed in, walking by us and toward the door.

Luca gently grabbed my upper arms. "I want you in here where it's safe."

"And that's not happening. I'm fighting by your side. No discussion."

We stood in a standoff for a few moments. I could see he was battling himself, but no way I was relenting. This was an all or nothing relationship. He wanted to live it real? An alpha pair fought together. If we didn't, there would be many questions over our mating. We had enough of those as it was and didn't need any more.

"We do this real," I whispered so softly only he could hear.

More thoughts trickled through his eyes. "Stay by me," he ordered.

I had no intention of doing that. If I was needed somewhere, I'd go there with no hesitation. One second too late ended up with someone killed.

We piled out of the house just as the wolves came into view. They were running full speed, their intent on attacking and nothing else.

One by one, we shifted into our animals. Luca's was beautiful with gray fur around his head and feet. The rest of him was a shiny black. Absolutely stunning. My wolf only had a moment to look because the fight was on.

A wolf with dishwater brown fur came charging at me, snarling and snapping her teeth at me. Due to the thin line of the nose, my wolf could tell it was a female. .

We went into an all-out battle. My wolf swiped our claws, getting a bit of the bitch's shoulder. Her howls of pain weren't enough to appease my wolf.

Her teeth came very close to my nose and gave off a snap. My wolf reared back, then went for the female's shoulder, clamping down violently. She struggled, trying to break free, but my wolf was strong. Stronger than most everyone gave her credit for.

When we shifted, our wolves were in charge. Our human self still thought and felt, but out wolf ran on complete instincts. It was why many wanted to be alphas, because they had the most control. My wolf had it leaps and bounds. Always had.

I felt the pain of my wolf's leg getting twisted as the other female wolf clawed in.

Off in the distance, I heard other wolves of my pack, which surprised me since we hadn't met. Nevertheless, my wolf detected one was in distress.

Summoning up my alpha strength, my wolf unleashed on the bitch, biting, snarling, and attacking until she ripped the throat from the female and left her down on the ground.

All of Luca's pack was fighting, and Natalie was in trouble. She looked to have an alpha male on her hands, judging by his unbreakable stance.

My wolf charged over and knocked the wolf away from Natalie and to the ground. It didn't take long for him to get back up and come at my wolf. He was powerful, but I didn't feel that he was the leader of this pack. Yes, he was an alpha, but he was missing something.

Natalie launched into the fight, as well. Two against one, we somehow found a way to work together.

He clawed and bit. It took a very tricky back arch to miss getting gutted wide open. Then my wolf latched on to the back of his neck, while Natalie went for his throat, pulling it out and spitting it to the ground.

Howls came from around us, and we looked around.

Luca and Jonas were still fighting. Where the hell had the other wolves gone?

The wolf on Luca had a strong hold of him with his teeth, and Luca was having trouble shaking him off.

My wolf charged forward, noting Natalie wasn't behind me, and nailed a white wolf with black on its front two paws and the tip of his tail. He, too, exuded alpha waves, so between the three of us, it was all-consuming.

We tumbled to the ground, and Luca's wolf became free.

My wolf moved back, perceiving this alpha was pissed as hell, showing me his teeth and adding in the drips of saliva down his jaw. His eyes were on my wolf, which was a mistake.

Luca charged him. In one fell swoop, he clawed the wolves gut, slicing him completely open. Luca didn't stop there. He then went for the throat, tearing it out, then decided he needed to play around with the dead animal.

Looking around, the wolves that had charged in were all down, and our wolves were all coming back.

Natalie was standing off to the side, just watching.

Pain ricocheted through my shoulder and paws.

When I fell over, Luca shifted, coming to me in a rush.

"Shift!" he yelled, and I listened, coming back to human form. His arms were around me, strong and comforting. "Shift back," he said again, and I did. We did this four more times before I finally stayed human. The magic within us healed our wounds, and the only way to let the magic to take over fast was to repeatedly shift. Sometimes when we're in that much pain, we forget. I was lucky Luca was there to help me.

"I'm good."

He smiled down at me. "Yeah, you're damn perfect."

CHAPTER EIGHT

"Hello?"

"Hey, Dad," I said into the phone as I laid on the bed I shared with Luca.

There's a rustling around on the other end of the phone like he's moving. "How's my little girl doing?"

Happiness filled me at his words. "Good. Really good."

"I'm happy for ya, baby girl."

"Dad, I've called Howls for the past few weeks, and every time I ask about my schedule, they tell me I don't have one." This had been bothering me for a while now, and my wishful thinking had come into play that my father was just giving me time to get settled in my new life. That wasn't the case. As time passed, I got the distinct impression I was being pushed out.

He sighed heavy. "It's best if you don't work there, and I got all the books handled."

"Dad!" I was in complete shock that I popped up from the bed and began pacing the room.

"You have a new family, and you need to concentrate on them. That's what a mate does, Caleigh. They leave their life behind and join the other pack, doing jobs for them. You know this."

"So, you're going to cut me out?"

"Out of our lives? No. Never. As for the business, it's best this way. And Caleigh, you know it."

My heart hurt. This was the severance I was terrified of, because of the bargain. My family had said they'd take me back, but would they really after this? Unfortunately, there wasn't anything I could do about it.

"Yeah. How's Wolf coming along?"

"Good. We're opening next week. Everything is great, Caleigh." Even though my heart hurt, happiness filled me at knowing I had helped my family. That I was able to fix the problems and let them live easy.

"I'm happy for ya, Dad." A lump caught in my throat, and I cleared it. "Can you tell everyone I said hi?"

"Absolutely. You'll have to come over for dinner sometime."

The lump grew. "Yeah, I'd like that."

"Gotta run now."

"Bye, Dad. Love you."

"Love you, too." He disconnected the phone, and I swiped mine off, tossing it to the bed.

My heart felt heavy, and it took everything I had not to let the sadness overtake me. My family was moving on, but I hadn't given them any other choice. Doing what's best sometimes sucked.

Even worse, in the weeks since I had first slept with Luca, the connection was so much stronger. I swore it'd only get stronger by the day.

"ABOUT TIME you got down here. You're gonna miss the food," Niko teased as Luca and I entered the dining room.

"Wouldn't kill ya to lay off the meat," I chided as he laughed.

"Never!" He piled a piece of hamburger into his mouth, chewing it with a smile on his face.

We got our own food then joined the masses at the tables, joining in on conversations and adding in our own.

One month and these people felt like family. We joked like my brothers and I joked. There was an easy comradery. Natalie didn't say anything to me, and I didn't care. She stayed away from me, and I stayed away from her. It was a good balance.

Luca put his hand on my thigh and gave it a squeeze, sending butterflies through my system. I loved having him near me.

"So, how's it goin'?" Sage asked, siding up to us.

We had made peace over why I was here and had become closer than we were before, if that was even possible. Living under the same room as her had been a blessing.

"Great! Luca's keeping me busy."

"I bet he is." She raised her brows suggestively then smiled.

I slapped her playfully. "Stop it. I mean, I've been helping him organize things in his office and get everything in line. There's a new computer program that makes keeping track of business dealings so much easier, so I'm transitioning everything to that."

This past week, I'd been working on this nonstop, and I loved it. It gave me a sense of purpose, making me feel as if I were contributing to the pack. I'd never want to be a mooch or sit up in Luca's room, eating bonbons and getting waited on hand and foot. That wasn't me. I was an action person, wanting to be in the thick of things. Luca gave that to me, including me more and more everyday into his pack.

It made me happy. He made me happy.

She leaned in close, whispering, "You're happy?"

I gave a soft nod and a smile. "Yeah."

"Good. That's all I ever wanted for you." She pulled me into her arms and hugged me.

"Love you," I said softly in her ear, and her embrace went a little tighter.

"Love you right back."

"OH, HEAVENS!" I cried out as Luca thrust deeper inside of me. I clutched the bedsheets, trying to keep myself upright, but I lost the battle and fell to my elbows.

With Luca behind me, pounding away at my pussy and clawing at my hips, the bed shifted with each movement, no doubt skidding across the hardwood floor.

"Take it," he growled harshly, pushing my back down to arch more. His hips were like the pistons of a steam engine, moving without pause. I could smell his arousal seeping off him, which only make me wetter knowing I was the cause of it.

He removed his hand from my hip and slapped down hard on my ass, making a *crack* resound through the room.

I came. That burst of pain had sent me flying over the edge, soaring.

My head fell to the bed, bouncing as he pushed as deeply as he could inside me. His body stiffened, and then he grunted. I could feel him come inside me.

It was bliss.

CHAPTER NINE

THE STORM ROLLED IN QUICKLY, NOT GIVING ANYONE much warning. Not even our wolves sensed it until it was closer than we had thought. Outside Luca's room—our room —was a balcony with a very comfortable chair and an awning over it. That's where I was sitting outside, watching the storm take over. Every rumble was beautiful and charged me with energy.

The door opened and Luca stepped out. "There you are. Still have a thing for storms, I see."

"You remembered."

He walked over, lifted me up, and sat in the chair, pulling me onto his lap with very little effort. I curled into him, resting my head on his chest.

"I love how you fit against me, beautiful."

My heart did that fluttery thing it had been doing every time Luca said or did something nice for me, which meant it happened a lot. He was always doing small things to let me know he was thinking about me. A small touch on my arm as he walked by while going to his office. A text that he was thinking of me. Picking me up on the couch and planting me on his lap while I watched television right in front of everyone. All of it was adding up and sinking deeper in my soul.

"Me, too," I replied just as a crack when off in the distance then the rumble of thunder shaking the world around us.

"I remember everything about you, Caleigh, never doubt that. You used to love to sit out and listen to the rain and never cared it was lightning so badly or so close it could have hurt you. You were strong and independent in your own mind, even at a young age."

"It's never changed," I said into his shirt, inhaling him and the rain, a magnificent combination, and one I never wanted to forget. Those strings between us tightened. Each time that I thought they couldn't get stronger, they proved me wrong.

"That's another thing I love about you—history."

"Yeah, like the time you covered my entire room with toilet paper while I slept, put shaving cream on my hand, and then tickled my nose."

He laughed. "You've always been a heavy sleeper. How about when you and Sage followed me and my buddies out to the lake just to watch us strip down."

I gasped. "We did no such thing." That was a total lie, but how the hell did he know that? We never told a soul.

"Smelled you, Caleigh. Knew you were there the whole time." I tried to lift up, but he pushed me back to his chest. "I like you here, and yes, it's true."

"Shit," I grumbled, knowing there was no use in arguing. He had caught me.

"Yeah, no shit."

The rain poured down, falling off the awning in waves. The thunder crashed, and lightning lit up the sky. All the while, I lay with my man, listening to him tell me all the things he knew I had done, even at a young age.

It was magical.

"RIGHT, so if you used this on a daily basis, when it comes time to look things up and organize them, we'll have a much better shot of not missing anything."

Luca listened intently to everything while I sat on his lap at his insistence, telling him my ideas. It didn't take much convincing, because I loved sitting there, close to him, connected. It was the time when I felt safest and secure.

"I want you to come in and handle it," he declared.

Blowing out a breath, my hair moved with it. "It would keep me busy."

He twisted me, pulled me to his lips, and kissed me. "I'll keep you busy." His lips attacked mine while I fully turned and straddled him in his office chair. It had slots on the sides where I threaded my legs through. Then I twisted his hair in my fingers the roughness of his face taking me away.

We drank each other in. My core clenched, and the more I rocked my hips against his hard length, the wetter I became.

He moved his hands underneath my arms and lifted me, placing me on the desk after pushing things off to the side.

"Luca," I breathed as he tore my shorts and underwear from my body, leaving my lower half exposed to him on his desk.

He sat back in his chair, grabbed my knees, and pulled me to the edge of the desk. Then his mouth was on me, taking with a hunger I'd only dreamt of making a man feel. It was wild, hot, and with each swipe of his tongue, or graze of his teeth, everything down there started to vibrate with need.

"Luca," I gasped when he pulled away, not wanting him to leave me because I was right there on the brink of a very intense orgasm.

I watched as he unzipped his pants, unbuttoned them, and then let them fall to his knees. He pulled out his beautiful cock, stroking it. A drop of pre-come came from the tip, and I itched to lick it off, but his face told me to lie back and take what he was about to give me.

Without taking his clothes off, he surged inside of me. My back and neck arched, and I clutched the desk as he fucked me without abandon. The desk shook, the computer wobbled, the room became so hot. I was afraid I just might pass out.

I felt his hand come to my clit, and then he rubbed it fiercely over and over, each time rougher, which sparked my orgasm.

Luca rode me out, then pulled my legs straight up in the air and pressed my thighs together, trapping his cock in my already pulsing flesh. That was when he let loose like only Luca could.

"Fuck, you're hot," he growled.

"Luca!" I yelled out, feeling the makings of another orgasm slam into me. All my word did was spur him on faster and harder.

Sweat trickled down his forehead as he closed his eyes, tossed his head back, and groaned out his release.

Damn, he was beautiful and all mine ... for now.

———————

CHAPTER TEN

"You have to get that!" Sage said, standing in front of me in the dressing room, where she had just had to get out of the house and shop.

For a while, Luca hadn't let any of us out of the house after the fight. He never did figure out why they had come after him and said he had found no connection.

The only thing he had found out from another pack alpha was there were some rogue wolves in the area who wanted territory. Luca had chalked it up to that, and then allowed us to get out. He was really protective, which was one of the things I admired most about him. He loved his family and took care of it in every aspect.

Now that Luca had let us out, feeling that everything was in the clear, Sage was ready to live it up. She even went as far as to pick out my clothes.

The top was cut short, hitting right at the top of the denim skirt. If I lifted my arms, I'd flash everyone my waist. The skirt was short, as well, coming to mid-thigh. There was no way I'd be bending in it.

"It's not practical, Sage. The only place I'd wear this is in the bedroom with your brother."

"Nah, they make better stuff for that." She waved her hand dismissively. "How about this shirt?" She pulled another from the rack, and I tried it on. It came down lower at the waist, but it was cut in a deep V in the front, showing the girls off and all their glory.

"No! That!" Sage practically screamed. "No arguments."

I sighed, liking the shirt, but not really knowing when I'd wear it. I was more of a jeans and T-shirt type of woman, instead of fancy. But maybe Luca would take me out on a date or something and I'd need to wear it.

"Fine."

She squealed with joy and clapped her hands.

"I'm tired. Can we go back?"

Her brows lifted. "They aren't expecting us back for another couple of hours. Let's live it up!"

"Babe, we've been living it up for most of the day."

"You just want to get back to my brother," she stated matter-of-factly.

It was true. The connection we had drew me to go and see him. It wasn't a lie, though. I was tired and ready to lie down for a while. Shopping always took a lot out of me.

"Let's go."

She smiled, shaking her head, and then we left.

Entering the house, greetings came from all around. The family bond here was strong on all ends.

"I'm getting something to eat," Sage said just as my stomach growled.

"That sounds like a plan."

We sat at the kitchen counter, inhaling some leftover

meatloaf from the night before. I swore meatloaf tasted better the second day, but that was just me.

"Anyone seen Luca?" I asked the room at large.

"Last I saw him, he was upstairs." This came from Gary, a pack member.

A smile grew on my face.

Hauling ass upstairs, I looked in the office, but there was no Luca. Opening the door to our bedroom next, I stopped dead.

Movement came from the bed, but the sheet blocked my view, except for the blonde hair poking out at the top.

"Luca, hurry up before she gets home," Natalie said, and my wolf snarled as anger mixed with shock enveloped me.

I turned and raced out of the room, down the stairs, happy I had my purse on me still and the car keys inside my bag.

That had been my one stipulation with Luca—no women in his bed. None. And he'd had her when I wasn't home to hide it.

Pain sliced though my heart at the betrayal. Two and a half months, I'd been giving this relationship everything. Living it real. And now there was a woman in his bed. A woman who despised me. At least now I really knew why. She wanted Luca. Lucky for her. She could have him. He had broken the bargain.

Charging through the living room, Jonas stepped in front of me, hands out. "Slow down, Caleigh. What's wrong?"

My wolf snarled, wanting to shift. I could feel her pushing to the surface. Fur was sprouting from my face and arms, and my nose was elongating. It took everything inside of me to hold her back.

"Move out of way," I growled from deep in my chest, the sound reverberating through the room.

"Caleigh, talk to me."

I stepped closer and snapped my teeth. "Get out of my way!" I screeched this time, and Jonas stepped aside, but that didn't mean that all eyes weren't on me.

I didn't have a lot of time. I needed to get in my car and get out of here quickly.

With a quick gait, I got out of there, got in my car, and took off like a shot, thankful that the smell of exhaust would cover up my scent a bit.

Fumbling through the center console, I swerved off the road a bit, but regained myself. I grabbed the spray that was only for emergencies and began to coat my body with it. It masked scents long enough for me to get the hell out of this town.

Holding on to the steering wheel at ten and two, the pain hit, and it hit hard. It felt like a knife stabbing me right in the heart, and I was bleeding all over myself. My soul tore in half and felt as if it were on fire. Tears slid down my face as racking sobs clamored deep in my chest.

I had fallen for him. He'd wanted me to live it real, and I had one hundred percent. Sad thing was, I had known this would happen. I had known I'd be shredded. I just never thought it would be because of another woman in his bed, or the betrayal I felt from him.

My cell rang, but I ignored it.

I couldn't go to my parents because I'd have to explain everything, and I didn't have it in me. I needed space and time to myself to gather my thoughts and figure out what to do next. Hell, I just needed to be.

Driving for hours, I pulled into a Holiday Inn. It took a bit of talking for them not to use my credit card, but an extra hundred bucks to the manager got me under radar. My dad hadn't raised a stupid woman. If I used my credit card, anyone could find me, and I didn't want to be found.

I fell to the bed, burying myself in the white comforter and pillows, and wept.

MY BODY STIRRED.

He kissed me fiercely. The pulse between my legs grew.

I popped up from bed, my body sweating and covered in a light sheen. My breath came in small pants as all the memories came back of the last few hours.

Lying back down, I went back to sleep.

FOR TWO DAYS, I'd ordered take-out from the local places who delivered and slept. I watched a few movies that I hadn't seen since I was a kid, and then slept some more. The reason for sleeping so much was because the pull to Luca wasn't as strong when I drifted off.

When I was lucid, the ties to him were so strong they were painful, pulling me, urging me to go to him. Find him and let him hold me to stop the tearing inside of me. The physical pain was enough, add in the emotional and I was a damn mess.

My phone had kept ringing and ringing, so I had turned it off, unable to deal with anything or anyone. Especially not Luca, who'd been a majority of the calls. Whenever his name had come up, the pain had increased.

My wolf was restless inside and really needed to run,

but I was in a town I didn't know well and couldn't risk letting her out. Needless to say, we weren't on good terms, so it was another internal battle I was facing.

I picked myself up and hauled it to the shower, wanting to wash off the sweat from the night before. Last night had been worse than the one before, but I didn't have the dreams last night that had warranted them.

The cold spray washed everything away, yet when I stepped out, a weird change came over my body. Heat flooded me, and an arousal like none other hit my core.

I doubled over from the intensity, holding on to the sink to catch myself from falling to the tiled floor.

The arousal was so intense the muscles of my abs constricted painfully.

Somehow, I managed to make it to the bed and lie down, curled in a ball with my arms around my middle.

My clit throbbed, and I maneuvered myself so I could touch it. One swipe, and I flew into an orgasm. It was nothing like the ones Luca had given me, but it was intense and helped relieve some of the pain.

That's when it hit me. Heat. I was going through heat. Shit. Of all the times.

Sometimes, I wondered if the Heavens above were playing tricks on me.

I turned, groaning into the pillow as another wave hit violently and fast. My mother had told me about going into heat, how your body changed and orgasms helped relieve it for only short times. She'd also told me that it only lasted about twenty-four hours, and considering a minute was like twenty-four hours, this was going to be a very long day.

CHAPTER ELEVEN

Every muscle in my body ached like I'd done an Olympic triathlon four times over. I was exhausted, but I needed food. Leftover pizza and Chinese wasn't cutting it.

Luckily for me, a rib joint down the road delivered and should be here any moment.

I was weak and hated it, but there was no getting over it. I'd thought over and over again about Luca and how he could have helped me through yesterday. Then I had kicked my own ass for even thinking it.

A knock came to the door. I grabbed my wallet and pulled out some bills. I was grateful that I had saved my money. It was proving useful right now.

Hand on the door handle, I froze, inhaled, and my wolf roused. We knew.

The Heavens were definitely playing games with me. I wasn't sure what I did in my life or past lives, but this ... this was just cruel.

My wolf's tongue wagged, and she turned around in excited circles. Me, my heart was squeezing painfully.

"Caleigh, let me in," Luca said from the other side of the door.

Inhaling again, I rested my head against the door as the tears welled up in my eyes.

He was my mate.

There was no question about it. While my heart was breaking, those webs that had formed grew solid. There was no stopping them. It was the way of our world. Not spending the rest of my life with my mate would kill, literally, because I didn't think I would be able to make it.

I was breaking.

Piece by piece, everything inside of me was crumbling.

How had a simple bargain turned out to be so much more than I had bargained for?

He was my mate. I could smell it. My wolf could feel it. Regardless of the heartache, she wanted him, and she wanted him now.

Finding all the strength I never had before, I muttered, "Go away." I didn't mean it, but I did at the same time.

Pressing my hand against the wood of the door, I could feel him. So close, yet so far away.

"Baby, you know I can't do that."

He felt it, too. The intensity of this was more than before. More than when he had bitten me and marked me. More than when he had held me securely in his arms while the rain poured around us. All of this was more. I hadn't thought that was possible.

"Just go."

"Baby, I wasn't in that bed. Hell, I wasn't in the house."

How he knew any of this, I didn't know. I just needed him to go away because it hurt too much.

"Please, I don't want to do this with a door between us. Open up."

"I can't," I whispered.

"You're the strongest female I know. Open it and let's talk this out."

"What's to talk about? Natalie was in our bed!" I yelled loudly, not caring who heard.

"Either open the door, or I'm tearing it down, Cal. Decide now and step back." His alpha tone came out loud and clear.

I couldn't fight the pull. I unlocked the door and pulled the chain. It opened immediately, and Luca stepped through in all his sexy glory.

Why on earth this man had to be so hot was beyond me?

He closed the door, his breathing ragged, his eyes looking tired.

I took several steps back.

"Baby, it was a setup. I was on the property, letting my wolf run with George. Jonas told me you ran out. He went up to our room and saw Natalie there. He kicked her ass out and came to find me. All of it was a setup." He stepped closer, and the back of my knees hit the bed as I moved away. I moved around it.

My heart squeezed and thumped. Everything inside me was telling me that Luca wasn't lying to me.

"You weren't there?"

Luca, hurry up before she gets back. Natalie's words rang through my head.

"No, baby. I would never cheat on my mate. Never."

"But, we weren't really mates." I shook my head, trying to clear my thoughts, but it wouldn't happen.

He came to me and placed his hands on my arms. They felt like sexy lava on my skin.

My wolf howled, wanting to consummate the mating. I

held her back, along with my raging body, which proved difficult with him this close.

"Six months ago, I went to an Oracle. I didn't ask her, but she felt the need to tell me who my future mate was. Luck was on my side when Sage told me what was happening, and I took the initiative to get you in my bed."

Eyes wide and mouth dropped open, I stared at the man in front of me. "You knew?"

"Yeah, baby, I knew, and I was so fucking happy when she told me. You've been on my mind for years, and when she gave me the news, I couldn't wait to have you with me and in my bed."

"Natalie set us up?"

An angry glint came to his eye. "Yeah, the bitch did, and she's in lockdown right now because I didn't want to deal with her. I wanted to find you. Unfortunately, you're too smart for your own good." His face changed at the last words, and a smirk played, then it turned serious. "Killed me deep in my soul that I couldn't find you. It was a pain I never want to live through again."

My head fell to his chest. "I'm so stupid."

Luca kissed my hair and pulled me into his arms. "No, baby. Damn, I can smell you went through heat. I'm just so damn sorry you had to go through that alone."

"I was so mad at you. So hurt." Tears welled in my eyes as the last few days came crashing around me. All the pain and devastation flooded me, and I felt my knees give out. Luca held me strong, letting me cry it out.

"I know. I hate that you were locked in this room, dealing with that and heat. It's why I wanted you in my bed early, so I could have eased your pain during the time. That didn't work out, it seems." He rubbed small circles on my back, comforting me.

"I'm in love with you," I said softly.

"Good, because I love you, too." He pulled me away then kissed me furiously, but with a passion that he'd been holding back on me. This was almost sweet in a way.

He walked us back to the bed, the back of my knees hitting it. We laid down, still kissing, still connected. My heart fluttered and swam, feeling so much at one time.

This time, he took his time. He stripped my shirt, then kissed every part of my exposed flesh, sending prickles along my skin. He removed my bra, then spent time on my breasts and nipples, sucking them into his mouth, then tugging them with his teeth. My body reacted, arching into his touch and following him when he left me even for brief periods of time when he stripped my pants, kissed down my legs, and my core.

Turned on wasn't even it. I was beyond that needing to be filled with him.

"Baby, please," I groaned as his head popped up, eyes intense and knowing.

Luca pulled away, stripping his clothes before climbing back on top of me, then sliding inside of me. I tried to arch, but with his weight, I didn't get far.

Luca laced our fingers together and rested them on either side of my head, his eyes connected to mine, burning into me so profoundly it wrapped around my soul, clicking our connection in place for all eternity.

As he made love to me, never taking his eyes off me, it was the single greatest experience of my life. When we came, we did it together, only solidifying it.

ENTERING THE PACK HOUSE, it felt like the first time

with all eyes on me, except there was deep concern this time, and it was aimed at both Luca and myself. I'd probably worried them with my disappearing act. Guilt slammed into me at the thought.

I gave a soft wave. "Hey. Sorry, guys."

Jonas came up and wrapped his arms around me. Luca growled, and he stepped back.

"So damn happy you're back."

"Thanks."

"I smell it," Jonas said with pride. "It's stronger than before."

I looked up to Luca who had a wide, happy smile. "Yeah, she's never leaving again."

Contentment filled me like no other.

"What are we doing with Natalie?"

At the mention of her name, my mood instantly changed, and my wolf wanted to get out, wanted to attack and protect what was hers.

Luca firmly wrapped his arm around me, sensing my struggle, another thing I'd come to learn about mates—being able to channel their feelings.

"I want to talk to her," I declared.

Jonas nodded, obviously understanding my tone.

Luca led me to a room I hadn't been in before, turned the outside lock, and we went in to find Natalie sitting on the small twin bed, her furious eyes coming to us. Luca tried to move in front of me, but I held a hand out, stopping him. This was between her and me, and it needed to be settled as such.

"Leave. You have one hour to pack your shit. You don't come back ... ever. You don't send a postcard to this pack. You don't phone. You don't exist for us ... ever. You don't do that, I take you out right here and now for deceitfulness, and I won't think twice about it."

"He's mine!" she growled.

I snarled back, "No, he's mine. So, does this mean you want your throat ripped out?" I shrugged like it was all the same to me.

"I have nowhere to go."

"And you didn't give a rat's ass that *I* had nowhere to go, either. Correct? Eye for an eye."

She looked to Luca, and I knew she was going to play the guilt card. I'd seen women like her all my life, always playing on their looks and vulnerabilities to get what they wanted in life. I wasn't having it.

"Save it. As alpha female of this pack, you either back down to me or we fight. I will not tolerate you in my space. You're lucky you're even getting a choice in the matter." She was. I should just take her out and be done with it, but she didn't physically do anything to me. She's just a betraying bitch.

The air became tense with a thickness that tried to weigh me down. I could also sense a small bit of fear coming off Natalie, but mostly, it was anger. Some wolves got set in their ways and wanted certain things. When they didn't get said things, they turned into selfish bitches like the one in front of me. They only wanted what they wanted, not caring about anyone else.

Her furious eyes came back to me. "Fight," she said.

I didn't waste time. I stripped, and my wolf came out.

The fight was ugly, bloody, and within minutes, my wolf had Natalie's throat in her mouth.

It was done.

I'd wanted to give her a chance to not fight, but deep down, I had known that's what she would choose. Luca believed in me and my abilities, not wanting me to look weak in front of the pack. He didn't stop it, because he'd known I could do it. That warmed my heart.

Now Luca and I could live free and happy, mated and in love.

EPILOGUE

2 YEARS LATER...

"Sabrina, Sal, Sarah, get back here right now!" I called out to my pups as they ran around the property, farther than they were supposed to go yet kept going, anyway. They were like that—triplets with minds of their own and always wanting to exert themselves. My parents doted on them, spoiled them, and when they came back to us, they were wound up.

Both Mom and Dad had been ecstatic when I'd told them I was pregnant, and even more so when they'd smelled my mate on me.

"Let them run," Luca said, looking out over the field as he put his arm around my shoulder. "They have to get that energy out."

This was true. We'd learned that kids were a handful. Active beyond belief and with all the sugar my parents gave them. The only one who's worse than my parents was Sage. She spoiled them, too, and loved them deeply.

She hadn't found her mate yet, and selfishly, I was happy she was still around to be with the kids. She's a strange phenomenon in our family because she hadn't gone into heat yet. She should have gone around the same time as me, but for some reason, it hadn't happened yet.

"Ever thought you'd have this life?" I asked, looking up at my mate.

"Knew we'd be happy. Knew we'd have everything we ever wanted. Knew I loved you. That's all that matters."

"Love you." I rose on my tiptoes and kissed his lips. He returned the favor.

Life was perfect, all because of a bargain. I couldn't have asked for more.

THE END

EXCERPT OF THE ALPHA'S ARRANGEMENT

Inhaling deeply, the crisp mountain air flows through my lungs, pure and refreshing. After living in the city for most of my life, coming here is an oasis. There are no sounds of cars, people yelling, or construction on buildings so high your neck aches to look up. Only the flit of a bird off in the distance and something wrestling in the trees can be heard. Peace. Calm.

I came to Spear to get away from the city. It's the complete opposite and beyond perfect. This perfection came at a steep price, though. The old owners wanted to sell, but only for their full asking price. Even with my lawyers haggling, they wouldn't budge, which I admire.

Seeing this place for the first time in person, it's understandable why they didn't want to give up this beauty. I'm not sure I ever could.

The home is large, much bigger than I truly need, but it screamed "home." That's what I need—a home of my own for once. Not moving from place to place, not seeing the world, but having some place steady.

With five bedrooms, six bathrooms, and a full basement,

cleaning will probably be my main activity for a while. The previous owners didn't leave the place a mess, but they did leave their stamp on each room. One that needs to be thoroughly remodeled.

Sucking in one more deep breath, I enter my home, shutting the sliding glass door behind me. Cleaning supplies and food are the top two things on the agenda. The realtor gave me a brief lay of the land after handing over my keys, stating, *"Main Street has everything you need—bakery, groceries, hardware, mechanic, and a couple of restaurants and bars. Not much, but it's enough."* Main street is where I shall go first.

The winding roads from my home into the town make me thankful that I traded in my car for a Jeep four by four. One flick of a switch, and she's ready to tackle whatever comes her way. With the winters, I have no doubt I'll need it. Montana doesn't have light snow normally, and I love that.

Several people walk down the sidewalks on either side of the street, almost giving it a city feel, except there are nowhere near as many people. Their eyes follow me as I move through town, no doubt wondering who the newbie is.

The realtor was definitely correct about the town having everything I would ever need. The grocery store looks quaint, with lit-up windows and people mingling around. Nothing like the supercenters—another great change of pace.

The sliding glass door opens as I enter before grabbing a cart. It isn't lost on me that, as soon as I push my cart through the second door, all eyes are on me. It doesn't bother me. Instead, a smile spreads across my face. I'll never know the people here if there's a scowl on my lips. This is my fresh start. My way of leaving the hustle and bustle behind and finding my happiness.

Coasting down aisle after aisle, I get a lay of the land, giving slight nods to those who stare. It would be nice if they would say hi or something, but that goes both ways.

Smiling, I go back to the canned soups, which I hate, and get the ingredients for my homemade chicken and noodles.

Each aisle goes by in a blur as I collect everything I'll need for the next week or so. Some of my furniture will be delivered tomorrow, and I really want to be a house potato for a while.

I've introduced myself to several more people before I make it to the meat section, when my breath catches. Two mountains of men stand with their backs to me. One has inky black hair, while the other has a lighter brown.

No sooner do I stop the cart and see them, they turn to me in unison, and that's when my lungs become deprived of oxygen.

Both men are gorgeous, but the one with the inky hair calls to me, with eyes that are a deep navy, looking almost black. Whoever his parents are gave him fantastic bone structure, a strong jaw, and a masculine nose. Not to mention his size that is only slightly bigger than the man next to him. The forest green, long-sleeved thermal he has on showcases each dip and valley of his muscular chest.

This town must have a gym, because there is no way these two men look like this without working out ... a lot.

Inky man sniffs the air, and I instantly feel self-conscious, but I dismiss it just as fast. He can't be sniffing me from that distance.

"Hi." I give a soft wave.

"Well, hello there," the brown-haired man says, taking a

step my way, but inky man throws out his arm, holding the other man back.

Brown-haired man's eyes snap to inky man.

"Mine," inky man growls in a deep, sexy as all hell voice. And while I feel that rumble all the way to my core, his word makes no sense.

"Pardon?" I shake my head, dismissing the comment. "Sorry, hi, I'm Iso ..." I stutter, making a quick decision. New life, new name. Isobel is going to stay back in the city. "Izzy. You can call me Izzy."

"Owen," the man with light brown hair says with a smirk, looking between inky man and myself.

I look to the sexy as sin male who is blatantly staring at me, not making any attempt to hide it. Something warm snakes up my body, causing me to let out a shiver.

Damn, girl, it hasn't been that long since you got any.

"Carter," he states firmly and with authority. "McCavitt house?" At least he proves my assumption about it being a small town where gossip is concerned.

"Yes."

"You get all your stuff moved in?" This question takes me a bit off guard, because it's not one of the normal ones I've been getting. *How do you like it here? Where are you from? Why did you move here?* Those are the normal ones. My stuff, not so much.

"Tomorrow."

His stance changes a bit. The once rigidness of his muscles relaxes, yet he carries himself with such authority that, if one wasn't looking, I'm sure it would have been missed. Carter is casual, but very much on alert for some reason, making me a bit nervous. Somehow, he must sense this, because he inhales and some of that alertness disappears, setting me at ease.

"What time? My men and I will come help you."

"That's really nice of you, but the movers will take care of it." Even if that is super sweet of him, there's no way I'd accept that kind of help from a stranger. It's too much.

"What time? We'll be there to help," Carter repeats, and Owen chuckles under his breath.

"What's so funny?" I ask, instead of answering Carter.

"Nothing, Izzy. I'm just happy you came to Spear."

Carter takes a step forward, moving to the side of my shopping cart so he's mere inches from me.

It's my turn to inhale him. The smells of wood, oak, a hint of leather, and testosterone-filled male come through loud and clear. It's an absolutely intoxicating concoction.

"What time?" he repeats yet again, not backing down.

"Ten." My response comes out before I can filter it, as if he's putting a wicked spell on me and sucking me under.

His white teeth make an appearance, and I fully admit that I'm a teeth woman. Something about when they sparkle turns me on. They don't need to be perfectly straight. It's just the color.

Damn.

"We'll be at your place at nine thirty. Do you want us to bring coffee?" A sexy glint comes to his eye.

"Really, you don't need to—"

"I insist. We help our own."

"Thank you, but ..." A single look from him cuts my words off. This one is different than the sexy one he gave me moments ago. This one is determined and leaves little room to no room to argue.

Carter brings his hand up and tucks a lock of hair behind my ear. All I can do is feel each featherlight touch and try my damnedest to continue breathing. Then he brings his fingers to my chin and holds me in place for a moment, almost like he is inspecting me. When he releases me, it's on a sigh.

"We must be going. We'll see you in the morning."

"Ah ... okay."

Carter takes one more look at me before Owen grabs the cart and pushes it off. I note that the only thing inside of it is meat.

Continue reading The Alpha's Arrangement: HERE

ABOUT THE AUTHOR

Ryan Michele found her passion in bringing fictional characters to life. She loves being in an imaginary world where anything is possible, and she has a knack for special twists readers don't see coming.

She writes MC, Contemporary, Erotic, Paranormal, New Adult, Inspirational, and other romance-based genres. Whether it's bikers, wolf-shifters, mafia, etc., Ryan spends her time making sure her heroes are strong and her heroines match them at every turn.

When she isn't writing, Ryan is a mom and wife, living in rural Illinois and reading by her pond in the warm sun.

Join my Reader Group: Ryan's Sultry Sinners

Come find out more:

www.authorryanmichele.net
ryanmicheleauthor@gmail.com

OTHER BOOKS BY RYAN MICHELE

www.authorryanmichele.net

Ravage MC Series:
    Ravage Me
    Seduce Me
    Consume Me
    Inflame Me
    Captivate Me
    Ravage MC Novella Collection
    Ride with Me (co-written with Chelsea Camaron)

Ravage MC Bound Series
    Bound by Family
    Bound by Desire
    Bound by Vengeance

Vipers Creed MC Series:

Crossover (co-written with Chelsea Camaron)
Challenged
Conquering
Conflicted (Coming soon)

Ruthless Rebels MC Series (co-written with Chelsea Camaron):
Shamed
Scorned
Scarred
Schooled

Loyalties Series:
Blood & Loyalties: A Mafia Romance

Raber Wolf Pack Series:
Raber Wolf Pack Book 1
Raber Wolf Pack Book 2
Raber Wolf Pack Book 3
Raber Wolf Pack Box Set

Standalone Romances
Full Length Novels:
Needing to Fall
Safe
Wanting You

Short Stories:
    Hate to Love
    Branded

Novella:
    Billionaire Up Romance
    Stood Up

www.authorryanmichele.net

The Billionaire Shifter's Secret Baby by Diana Seere
   Grab more info on the Author's Website HERE.

Royal Dragon's Baby by Anya Nowlan
   Grab more info on the Author's Website HERE.

The Werebear's Unwanted Bride by Marina Maddix
   Grab more info on the Author's Website HERE.

Hunted by the Dragon Duke by Mina Carter
   Grab more info on the Author's Website HERE.

The Billionaire Werewolf's Witch by Celia Kyle
   Grab more info on the Author's Website HERE.

The Wolf's Royal Baby by Milly Taiden
   Grab more info on the Author's Website HERE.

Her Scottish Wolf by Theodora Taylor
   Grab more info on the Author's Website HERE.

The Alpha's Arrangement by Ryan Michele
   Grab more info on the Author's Website HERE.

Falling for the Werewolf by Abbie Zanders
    Grab more info on the Author's Website HERE.

Her Unbearable Protector by Reina Torres
    Grab more info on the Author's Website HERE.

The Billionaire Dragon's Secret Son by Harmony Raines
    Grab more info on the Author's Website HERE.

The Big Bad Wolf's Ex by Tonya Brooks
    Grab more info on the Author's Website HERE.

The Alpha's Enemy Mate by Jessie Lane
    Grab more info on the Author's Website HERE.

EXCERPT OF THE RABER WOLF PACK BOOK ONE

Prologue

Looking in the oval mirror of my great-great grandmother's vanity, I pucker my lips then smoosh them together, making sure the shimmery gloss is perfectly distributed. Swiping the excess off with my index finger, I focus on my eyes, checking that every single one of my long, mascara-covered lashes are in place. I hate clumps that make me look like a freak.

My ice-blue eyes are surrounded in a smoky gray shadow, and I used way too much eyeliner. Still, the effect turned out pretty hot, making my eyes the focal point of my face. A good thing considering I was initially going for the no-foundation look tonight, until the pimple on my chin told me that wasn't going to happen. I tried just covering the spot and blending, but it looked like a caked mess of shit and

I had to start all over. Of all the days for my face to blow up and sprout nastiness, it had to be today.

My best friend Masie had talked me into sneaking out of the house for 'the party of the year,' or so she called it. I'm weighing a lot on tonight. If my father catches me, I'm screwed. To say he's overbearing is an understatement. He's protective to the tenth degree and keeps me firmly under his wing, but I know he does it out of love. But, most of the time it sucks. He scares off every male wolf that comes around. With him being Alpha of our pack, I have yet to find a male that will stand up to him when it comes to me. No one has had the balls yet. Pathetic really.

The worst of it is, I'm horny. Seriously, I've gone without sex for way too long. Us wolves are sexual creatures and we crave that—no, *need* that release. I've masturbated so much I had to buy a new vibrator about a month ago. If I get laid at this party, it will be all worth it.

Sure, my father will yell at me if I'm caught, but that should be the bulk of it. He'll just be happy that I'm home and safe. So, I'm taking the risk.

The distinct smell of my best friend floats through the air. "Bitch, are you ready yet?" Masie calls from the doorway of the bathroom, peeking her head in, knowing she didn't surprise me. One great thing about being a wolf is our heightened senses—smell, hearing, and sight are extremely powerful. My father thinks we are hanging out over at Masie's house for the night and he's gone on pack business, so this works out perfect.

"I'm coming, wench, hang on." I run my fingers through my auburn hair. I added a few curls, which have softened into awesome cascading waves, flowing down to just above my waist. I give one more fluff before turning toward her.

"Fucking shit, Zara. Hello! Bitch in heat, here." She

waves her hand in the air, laughter ringing in her voice, and I can't help but join her.

"I am. Let's go." Hell yes, I am, no argument here. I stand, adjusting my clothes in the full-length mirror. My bright blue, tight-as-shit skirt stops mid-thigh, and my black chiffon see-through top hangs off my shoulder. Underneath, I'm wearing a very boob-flattering tank that pushes my girls up for maximum cleavage.

"Damn, girl, you have got to let me borrow that outfit. Not that my tits or ass would look as good as yours, but I want it." Masie has been my best friend since birth, and she has given me shit about what she calls my 'lush assets' since I got them. I have tits and ass, big whoop. It means nothing. Not in our culture. *Smell* is the only thing that matters. If the person looks good, that's a bonus.

"Maze, you need to stop with that shit. You are beautiful so shut the fuck up." Another line I've probably repeated about a zillion times over the course of our friendship. One thing that seriously pisses me off about my best friend is her opinion of herself. She's always finding something wrong, when there is absolutely nothing there. It's because she hasn't found her mate yet. She's twenty-three, like me, but all of her sisters—twenty-one, twenty, and nineteen—have already found their mates. With her being the oldest and not having found *the one*, it kills her inside. Masie thinks she has some defect that makes her scent unappealing. She's dead wrong.

Whenever we do go out, the males flock to her. They just don't have the scent she's searching for. And she looks hot tonight. Sexy black hair, sultry makeup. Her black skirt is the length of mine, but nowhere near as tight. Her long-sleeved top has cutouts on the shoulders, and a deep, plunging V in the front. It pushes her boobs up, too. I love it.

She may not find her mate, but there's no doubt she'll get some.

"I didn't see anyone else here when I came in," she states.

"Nope, all away on pack business. We are sleeping at your house. No harm, no foul," I reply, smacking my lips.

"All right then, let's go. We don't want the good ones to be taken."

Hell, even if they have already screwed a female, it doesn't mean they are done. Most male wolves can orgasm multiple times in the course of a night. Some can go multiple times in one session. Yes, please.

"After you." I grab my four-inch heels, black with shimmery blue at the very tip of the toe, and slip them on once we get down the two flights of stairs in my house.

Tonight is going to be one hell of a night.

Chapter One

Life is so fragile, even for immortals. One night was all it took for mine to change.

As pain surges through my body, I'm reminded of this very thing. Death would be better than this, but he won't end me. I'm too important to his master plan. I didn't want him to succeed, but as the months come and go in a blur of hurt and punishment, I feel myself doing the one thing I never wanted.

Breaking. Bending to his will.

On that fateful night I received my powers from the Heavens, when my Nana O told me that I was destined for great things, a higher purpose in this life, she didn't mean this. She couldn't have imagined that this would be my fate.

I scream as the man who is supposed to love me pushes a long, steaming hot, metal rod into my stomach. The smell of my burning flesh enters my nostrils and pain floods every cell of my body. I wait, hoping for relief, but even as he removes the rod, it doesn't come. If anything, it gets worse, more intense. The worst part of all of this is he can do this for the rest of eternity if he chooses. Death will never come for me.

No, Nana O could have never meant this.

Ian pulls me onto his lap, wrapping his arm protectively around me, as any mate should do. He even growls as one of the other wolves looks my way appraisingly. He should get an Oscar for his stellar performance. This one, though, is definitely above and beyond his call of duty. Nothing like my fake mate taking it to another level in order to impress.

Alpha Ty and his Beta, Gregor, sit at the long, sleek wooden table in the conference room. I call him Alpha because father is too nice of a name for him. The pack enforcers are seated around the table as well, as I sit with Ian off to the side by the far wall. Here, but not here. Observing, but not part of the meeting. Not that I want to be. I'd love to be far away from this place, but that's not an option for me.

A mediator from the Wolf Council, which Alpha pays off, sits at the head of the table to preside over this sham of a meeting. One to supposedly create an alliance between the two packs, but it's all a big façade. Nothing is as it seems, exactly like my life.

The Ren Pack sits on the other side of the table,

assessing each of our wolves, eyeing them with curiosity and suspicion. They should. Our Alpha has been calling meetings like this for the past couple of weeks, meetings that have only one conclusion—deaths, and none from our pack.

Wolf packs are slowly dwindling, becoming non-existent, because our Alpha is taking out the highest wolves from each pack. While he's here, the rest of the pack is at the Rens' compound, completely wiping them out, killing everyone there. Leaving no one to report what my Alpha is doing. No one to warn others. Our kind is slowly meeting its demise, all at the hands of *him*.

But that's what he wants. To rule. Have power. All it is, is greed plain and simple.

Alpha has always been power hungry, but only to the point of being the pack's alpha. Never, while I was growing up, did he ever give any indication that being Alpha wasn't enough. He was always around, teaching and prepping me for whatever my future might hold, and he always kept a close eye on me. He's made sure that I didn't stray too far from the pack. I thought that it was because he loved me. He was protecting me from all the bad in the world. But I was mistaken. Horribly so.

I sniff the air and notice a subtle shift from light and fresh to dark and musty. One of our wolves is seated next to the Ren alpha, his lip twitching, his nostrils flaring in and out. Low growls rumble through the air around us, thickening the tension in the space. I lick my lips and taste the change in the room. It's as if the once-breezy climate has swirled into a thunderstorm ready to erupt, and the warning reverberates through my body.

My pathetic job is to use my gift, my ability to listen to other wolves' thoughts, to find out if the Ren pack has reinforcements outside. Or if they even have a clue that they are about to be obliterated. Alpha looks over to me, brows raised expectantly. With a simple shake of my head, I silently feed him the answer he seeks. None of the other members of their pack are waiting outside; none of the men back at their home base have contacted anyone here for help, which means our other enforcers are cleaning up there. This is the moment I always dread. Each time I'm forced to do this, it's a hard, black strike against my immortal soul. The darkness claws at my insides, but I can't escape it. It's a mark that can never be erased. A scar that will never heal. I should never have been put in this position. Ever. I fear there will never come a time when I can come back from it.

"Challenge," Alpha calls out, and arrogance and smugness drip from that one little word. Inside the other Alpha's head is a mix of surprise and disdain, but no fear. Never show fear, that's what Alphas do. "Outside," Alpha declares, after a bit of a stare down.

They file out, leaving me alone with Ian and the Councilor. If we are anywhere outside of the grounds of our pack, Ian or someone is with me to watch my every move, like I'd even try to escape. I've thought about it, don't get me wrong, but there is no way out. The chains are too tight around my neck, tethering me to his will.

I'd rather be dead.

This is my life, my pathetic, miserable, unfulfilled eternity of life. I need to learn how to survive it because he told me he'd never allow me the peace of death. So, instead I am *mated* to someone who really can't stand me and have learned to accept being a pawn for Alpha and the pack. It's either survive and do as I'm told or... I shake my head from the thought as goosebumps rise on my skin. I can't go back there, I won't.

I say nothing as I sit, quietly waiting for it to all be over so we can go back home. I use the term *home* loosely. I'm required to stay with Ian on my parents' level of the main house. Ian and I share the same bed nightly and attend all pack functions together, including meal times. All packs believe that we are actually mates. I shake my head at the thought.

"I said I'd do it." My voice comes out raspy because my throat is so damn dry. I can't remember the last time I had water. My entire body aches, even my fingernails and the ends of my hair. It's been so long. So damn long.

"Take this." My father holds out a large yellow and orange pill. I stare at it, willing it to disappear. I just know that it's poison, but not the kind to kill me, the kind to torture me. "I said take it," he growls, less patient than a few minutes before.

I've already decided my fate. With a shaky hand, I reach out and take the pill from his outstretched one, careful not to touch his skin. He holds out a bottle of water and I take it hungrily.

"No!" he barks as I start unscrewing the lid, and I freeze. "The pill first, then you can drink the rest." I lift the pill to my dry, cracked lips, and place it on my sandpaper-like tongue. I press the water to my mouth and try to swallow the pill. I gag as it gets stuck in my throat, cutting off my air supply. "You stupid female. Drink!" he screams, and I do, dislodging the pill from my throat. I stare at him with the water still in my hand. I long to actually drink it, just to feel it going down my throat. That last sip didn't feel like anything but more pain. "What are you waiting for? Drink."

I lift the bottle with both of my trembling hands, afraid that I may drop it. I can't waste any of this water. I don't have any idea when I will get more and dehydration is eating at me. I down the contents in a hurried rush, my stomach churning with it. Way too much, way too fast. I fear that everything I just drank is coming up hard.

"You do not throw up," he orders and I choke down the bile forming in my throat. Please stay down, please stay down.

He leaves the room, only to come back a few hours later. I pray this will be the time that he lets me free. "You want to know what you just swallowed?" I don't want to know actually, but it is not really a question; he'll tell me anyway. "You now have a mate. With my pack. That pill will bind your scent to his, ensuring you smell like mates, and no one will dispute it. Now you can never fucking leave."

I want to cry, sob, and scream. I want to throw something at this monster. A mate. So, I'm stuck here. This can't be true. It just can't.

"Don't fight it, Zara. It's done," he says before turning and leaving the room again. I fall to the floor and curl into a ball, wrapping my arms around my legs. No...just no.

It's utterly disgusting the torture that Alpha continues to dole out on a daily basis. Like all of the other shit that he did to me wasn't enough.

The Councilor's eyes focus on us as Ian's hand trails up and down my thigh. I feel nothing. No spark. No want. No trembles. No tingles in regions that should have them. Ian's hot—longish blond hair, deep brown eyes, muscular frame— but he doesn't do anything for me. His smell is totally wrong and turns my stomach with each sniff. It isn't even slightly enticing, and the farther his hand goes up the more I want to vomit. Neither Ian nor I can smell the mating, just everyone else around us.

I push my wolf back down as she whines, shaking her head in despair. Aware of the Councilor's watchful eyes, I don't want him to sense the turmoil rolling around inside of me. My wolf is still very much present, but she has gone into a state of hibernation, only waking when it's necessary. Like at one of these meetings or when I'm required to shift with the pack. Other than that, I don't hear a thought or feel a movement from her. She only sleeps.

'*Damn she's hot.*' The Councilor has no idea that I can hear his internal dialogue. '*What I wouldn't give to fuck her.*' I clench my hands into fists, trying to block out his thoughts, but they keep coming at me, each one dirtier than the last. '*I'd bend her over, ass up high, face down, and pound that pussy until she howls.*'

My stomach rolls and vomit climbs up my throat. I choke it down. My only saving grace is that he can't utter a word out loud. If he did, Ian would have the right to rip out his throat. The bastard would do it too, just because he can.

'*Done,*' I hear Alpha voice inside my head as he speaks the same ones to Gregor. Since learning of my *gift,* as he calls it, I've learned how to tune in to one being and shut out the others around me. I've become so adept at hearing people that they don't even need to be in the same room for me to know what they are thinking. It comes and with Alpha, it's as if he has a direct link to me. Even hearing his thoughts, before he addresses anyone as he speaks.

Honestly, I can't stand it, or him for that matter.

"It's done. Let's go." I rise from Ian's lap, brush his hand off me, and move toward the door. Ian grabs my hand as I go. Gotta keep up pretenses, right? I don't fight it because... what's the use? I'm stuck.

The copper smell of blood infiltrates my nostrils as I step outside and walk through the massacred wolves lying on the ground. All six that were in the room are torn to shreds. Alpha and Gregor slip on their shirts and we head to the black SUV waiting for us. Clean up is for the enforcers to deal with later.

I climb into the very back, Ian by my side. Alpha and Gregor sit in the middle row while two enforcers take the front. I stare out the window, not saying a word, only here physically. I shut down all thoughts from others and try to find some kind of solace, but it doesn't come.

"You did good, girl." Alpha's praises mean shit to me. They are nothing but a pat on his back for another task done dutifully by me. I stopped caring the moment more wanting power outranked taking care of his family, his daughter. The coldness in his eyes that first time I rejected his plan still haunts me.

"Daddy, we can't do this," I plead, tears streaming down my face and crashing to the cold floor beneath me. I can't take someone's life just for the hell of it.

"You'll do what I fucking say or you'll stay in there," he barks, and my hands grip the metal slats of the cage he locked me in moments before. The space is small, and all I can do is either sit or curl in a ball. Wolves are not made to be confined. We are born to be free, roam free. This...this can't be happening.

"Why do you want to hurt the others? We have been so happy for so long." I appeal to his more human side, or at least I try. In all my years, he's never shown me this side of him. Angry, menacing, cold.

"You've no idea what is going to happen, but I do. You'll

work for me so it doesn't. You will do as I say or you'll remain locked in here."

A low whimper escapes my throat. Where's my mom, surely she wouldn't let him cage me up like this. Would she? And my brother? Where is he?

"Daddy, please," I beg, unable to stop the sobs this time, and my chest constricts with the thought of him leaving me like this. He can't.

"You made your bed." He turns off the light in the small basement room and walks out of the door, locking it behind him. Panic hits me like a boulder to the gut. No, please no.

I learned quickly that disobeying him would not be tolerated. I never in a million years would have thought my father could allow such deep greed to overtake him. That his pack would now fear him instead of respect him. I don't know him at all. The man I loved when I was a pup is dead and has been since I revealed my power. The only connection I have to this wolf in the vehicle with me is that he is my Alpha. Just as the man I once knew is dead, so is a piece of me. A part of me died inside that cage. I did what I could, but I couldn't stay locked in there.

"Thank you, Alpha." I keep my voice monotone, withholding any emotion. I placate him and give him what he wants; in turn, he and the others, except for my on-duty bodyguard, stay away from me on the property. Not that it's any better, but at least I have a sliver of peace and I'm not completely locked up.

"Only three more to go." A smarmy smile spreads across Alpha's face, menacing evil emanating from it. It's detestable and if I were powerful enough, I'd rip his throat out myself. Wolves honor their Alphas and treat them with the utmost respect, but I have no interest in that. To me, my Alpha has no honor. He doesn't deserve respect.

"Daddy, please no!" I scream loudly, the sound bouncing off the walls of the small room. The fear is so thick I swear I'm in a fog.

"You always were fucking stubborn. Do I need to bring your mother and brother back in here?"

I still and shake my head adamantly. The last time he brought them down here, he beat them while I watched. I screamed for him to stop, pleaded, but he didn't. My mother got it bad, but my brother, Zane, got it worse. At one point, I thought for sure he was dead, but my father brought in the healer and healed him in front of me.

"No...no..." I repeat, somewhat controlling the tremor in my voice.

"Are you ready to do as I say?" He stares at me with eyes that are so cold, I'm surprised ice doesn't form around them. No warmth. Void. Emotionless. Gone.

But I can't do what he wants me to do. I can't. "No."

"You are a stubborn fool." He's asked me the same thing every day for Heaven knows how long. I've held myself together, I don't know how, but I have. Unfortunately, part of me is beginning to crack. I feel it in my bones. Daily the fracture grows deeper, threatening to break. I'm terrified that the damage will be irreparable. What would happen then?

"One week. I'm calling the Raber Pack to set up a meeting with Xavier. They are tough so we need to be extremely prepared." Alpha's voice pulls me out of my treacherous memories. Ironic, the man who gave me the memory is the one to pull me from it.

Alpha and his men carry on conversations like this all of the time, like I'm not even in the van with them. I've learned a lot by listening, but it's not like I can do anything with the information. I file it all away, like everything else, just sitting there useless for another day.

"They are younger wolves so we'll need to double up on the enforcers when we ambush. We'll need the women, too. They'll need to help at their pack house," Gregor chimes in, like it's nothing in the world to take out an entire pack in the blink of the eye. True, our kind have been challenging each other for centuries, but not like this. Not this deceitfully and disgracefully. At least before, the wolves could hold their heads up high, with us, no way. Our heads should hang down in shame. Challenges were honorable and fair. This is flat-out murder.

"Zara, can you get a read on them before the meeting?" Alpha asks, turning around in the seat. His once-dazzling eyes that I loved looking into as a child now hold nothing but hate. I focus on his stare, not backing down.

"I've never seen them so I cannot conjure up their thoughts," I reply, with zero emotion.

"So, if we can get you a picture, can you do it?" he asks, hopeful.

"I've tried and it doesn't work. I have to physically see them in order to hear them." I have answered this exact question a slew of times and each time, it's the same answer. He knows my powers don't work the way he wants them to and I wonder why he continually asks.

"Shit," he growls. "Somehow we need to get her in contact with at least the Beta and Gamma. I don't want to chance her seeing the Alpha," he announces to everyone in the car, everyone but me. I find this statement a bit odd considering I'm around Alphas at his little meetings, but I could not care less. His reasons are his own and he'll never share with me. Maybe if I get close enough to the other pack they might rip my throat out and save me from this. Maybe then I could find peace.

"They have a decent-sized pack," Gregor states, rubbing his chin, deep in thought.

"I want as few wolves as possible around Zara," Alpha warns. I'd love to roll my eyes, but I don't. I sit here quietly. Even though I do his bidding, he never wants me around other wolves unless it's absolutely necessary. Because heaven forbid I find my true mate and try to leave the pack. I scoff at the thought.

Everyone thinks I'm mated to Ian. I played along at the ceremony, even bit him, but felt nothing—no cosmic electrical connection, or whatever is supposed to happen when wolves mate. It was only a bite. Other wolves stay away from mated females and since I took that stupid little pill, they keep their distance from me. I can't blame them. Somehow, it tricks them just like everyone else. The emptiness inside of me leaves little hope that my true mate is even in existence any more. I should be able to feel something, but instead there is nothing there for my true one.

"Meeting in my office after dinner and we hash this out," Alpha orders. "Zara, you're not needed at the meeting." Of course I'm not, not that I would want to go. His words just prove that I'm insignificant, a peon.

"Thank you, Alpha," I reply lamely, ready to go to my room and be alone. Ian may sleep in the same bed as me, but his stuff is elsewhere in the house. He tries to stay away from me any way he can, but that is just not possible. He has to keep up the farce for his own position in the pack.

His role used to be a low-level enforcer, and he was never going to move higher up in the ranks. So, at Alpha's request, *for the sake of the pack,* he mated with me. I really don't know the details of what happened between him and Alpha. What I do know is, Ian came out of that meeting pissed the hell off, but ranking under my father at number four in the pack. He's now Alpha's duty guard and mine as well. So began my life of un-blissful mating.

Chapter Two

We pull up to our massive compound, the driver nods at the gatekeeper and he opens the enormous metal gates for us to enter. Our pack has spared no expense regarding protection. The tall walls surrounding the property are made of concrete and have electric charges at the top. The home is huge, overdone, and not compatible with the way wolves are supposed to live. This is lush, eccentric, modern: straight lines and stainless steel and black everything. It is actually, not a home at all. It's a showcase. For who, I'm not sure. Only the wolves in the pack are allowed inside. It's not as if we're having parties and inviting everyone on the planet over to show it off.

The SUV stops and we pile out. I set off quickly in my heels, wanting to be alone, needing space. None of the males follow step and from Ian's thoughts, he's thankful that I'm leaving. As I enter the house, smells of roast beef fill the air, but it only makes my stomach twist. I try my damnedest to miss meal times, but my presence is requested so I must show, smile, and keep my mouth shut. I consume what my body will handle and leave as quickly as possible.

"Zara." My name being called from the kitchen as I step on the first stair toward my solace stops me in my tracks. My mother, the Alpha female of the pack. *Damn*. I once had the kind of mom that would bake cookies with you and fix your scraped knee. I had a mother that I could talk to about anything and everything. I had all of that and in the span of a few months, it disappeared. Of course, my father beat it out of her and no one in the pack stopped him. I could say it's not her fault, but I'd be lying. I do blame her. She was supposed to protect me. That was her job as my mother. Now, after all this time has passed, I feel nothing for her, not even in the furthest recesses of my soul, some minute space, it's gone. Her lack of protecting me is unforgivable.

"Yes, mother," I answer with the same tone I address anyone from my pack. Clean, respectful, to the point and with the least amount of words possible.

"Would you like to come into the kitchen and help me out?" Her cheerful tone does zip to change my feelings toward her. Inside her mind, she's squirming, trying to find some way to make up for what happened to me. Trying to find some way to get me back, to get me to look at her the way I did when I was a kid. News flash, it will never happen, not in this lifetime, which is a long-ass time.

"I'm rather tired from today's meeting. I feel the need to lie down," I reply, looking directly into my mother's eyes. '*I wish you'd forgive me. I'm so sorry, sweetheart. I wish things were different.*' Apologies flutter through her mind and she knows I can hear them, but I make it a point to not give her the satisfaction of a response.

With my mother being the Alpha female of the pack, she should exert that authority on me, but she doesn't. Alpha females, normally, rule every other female in the pack, but with us, it's different. While I'm respectful to her, she has so much pent-up guilt for not helping me that she allows me to do my own thing. Other females in the pack have noticed this, and my mother has been challenged because of it several times. But she won those battles, remaining the top female.

I also know that my father has commanded her to leave me be, but my mother would have done that on her own. It's another small reprieve. I have so few of them and I cherish each and every one.

"Sure. Dinner will be in two hours. See you then." She wipes her hands on a towel nervously, which is kind of funny when you really think about it. Alpha female, nervous? Whatever, I don't have the energy to think about it.

"Thank you, mother," I say as I turn and make my escape to my room. I lock the door, giving myself an ounce of privacy, not letting it faze me that every wolf living here has a key. I kick off my platinum heels, take off my light gray skirt, and white blouse. I throw on my comfortable clothes, black yoga pants, and an old *Margaritaville* t-shirt. I enter my attached bathroom and avoid my eyes in the mirror. I just can't. When I look at myself, I have to face what I've helped Alpha do. It's better to keep avoiding it. Keep feeling nothing.

I grab a cleanser wipe and scrub all the makeup off my skin. I brush my teeth, trying to rid the bad taste today left in my mouth, and then twist my hair up into a messy bun, pulling a hair tie around it.

I fall into the bed and look up at the ceiling. Quiet, peace. All the voices are turned off, nothing clouding my head, leaving only me.

I royally suck.

I had such high expectations for myself. Such high

hopes. My parents were overprotective but not horrible while I was growing up. I thought I'd meet my mate and there would be this instantaneous, heart-stopping moment where we would be the only ones in the whole world. That everything would pause and the only focus would be on our connection. I had visions of my heart beating in sync with the man I was supposed to be with and talking to him through the mating link. I wanted that connection and more importantly, I wanted love. That absolute, unconditional love that only exists in human fairytales. Yep, that kind of love.

I was going to have a claiming ceremony filled with love and devotion. We would mark each other and be together until the end of eternity. We would have lots and lots of hot sex that would result in a ton of pups running around and be...happy. I'd be happy.

Instead, I am this. A shell of the strong, independent, take-no-shit-from-anyone woman that I used to be. I loved those things about myself. I was proud of them. I had confidence and even thought I was pretty. I had ambition and dreams.

It's amazing how all of *me* was destroyed. Now, I'm nothing. Alone. With each day that passes, I chastise myself for trusting him. Distressing thoughts constantly flitter through my head. Unable to stop them when I'm asleep, nightmares consume me. If only he would have given me death, then I could at least have peace.

The emptiness in my soul tightens, and knots form in my gut. What's left of my failed heart shrinks more and parts chip off, swirling into the abyss of nothingness. The hope that I once held so dear is shredded and set aflame, dissipating forever. Wetness forms behind my eyes. I will not cry. I will not shed one more damn tear on the poor, pitiful me train. I choke it back and breathe in deep, fighting the emotion with everything I have.

I look up at the ceiling, counting the intricate circles that someone took so much time painstakingly engraving into the worn ceiling. No one in my pack probably even notices. But they have become a lifeline for me these past months. Counting them one by one in order to get away from all of the thoughts in my head, those of mine and those of others. Counting, slow and methodical, until my eyes begin to close and I drift off.

Tired. Alone. Caged. Constricted. Restricted. Hopeless.

A sharp clang rings out. Steel metal bars encase me from top to bottom, leaving only a cold metal floor, where I lie naked. I jolt from the noise. Please not again. Please not again. I've been holding on to what little sanity I have left for quite some time. How many days, I have no idea. They all blend together at this point.

Stubborn, my father calls it. Disrespectful. Unappreciative.

"Get your ass up," he yells into the cage. I try to obey, but my body is so weak, so tired. It takes a bit, but I push myself up on my hands and knees, panting with each move. Not having regular food and water, especially when you're a high metabolism wolf burning food faster than one can consume it, is disastrous. I rise to my feet, ever so slowly, legs trembling from holding my weight as I grasp onto the metal bars.

"Why are you doing this to yourself, Zara? Why put yourself through this? Just say yes and all of this will be over." My father's voice echoes throughout the room.

I can't give up. There is still hope, hope that my father

will see that he is wrong. He wants me to be his puppet. I can't be part of that. I don't want anyone killed.

"So, what is it today? Yes, you'll do what I say, or no and you're still trapped?" Being trapped is horrendous. Being trapped in this confined space is inhumane. And the male standing before me that was supposed to love me unconditionally, did this to me. He left me to rot in my own feces and piss. I will not let him win.

"No." My words come out croaky from lack of water and little to no saliva coating the inside of my mouth. My body is changing. What once was curves and luminous skin is now dull and bony. My hair. My beautiful hair. Chunks of it have fallen out, fluttered to the filthy ground.

"Fine, suit yourself." My father picks up a metal rod. I've never seen it before and have no idea what it is. Panic and fear paralyze me. He picks up the end of it and electric currents wiggle back and forth from two spikes coming out of the sides. Holy shit. "You did this to yourself, and you have no one to blame but yourself."

The rod inches closer and closer. I try to move to the corner of my small box to escape, but there is no use. The rod pierces me...

Ahh...holy shit. I wake with a start, sitting up on the bed and looking around to make sure I'm not *there.*

Bed. Curtains. Vanity. Bathroom. Check.

My heart is racing and I will it to slow down by breathing deeply. I'm fine. I'm not there any more. I'm not in physical pain any more.

I wipe my hands over my face and thread them through my hair. Nightmares. I have them every time I close my eyes and try to fall asleep. They come at me like a raging bull over and over again, knocking me on my ass each time, and leaving me back in that place. I wish I could wipe it from my head, make it go away just for one night of peaceful sleep.

It doesn't surprise me that I zonked out. I hardly sleep at all now. Usually, only when I'm so exhausted that it pulls me under. I hate sleeping because it leads to dreams and each time I wake up from one, I hate my father more. I hate him with every cell in my body. I hate what he has become. What he has made me.

My hands start to throb and I realize I've balled up the blankets on my bed and am squeezing them hard enough for my knuckles to turn white. I quickly release them, not wanting to rip the fabric, and thanking the Heavens that my claws didn't extend.

Inside, my wolf cries. When I was captured, she came out fighting, but my father shot me full of tranquilizers, debilitating my wolf and not allowing her to come out. As time went on, the tranquilizers were cut and my wolf's restlessness was making me even crazier. At one point, I thought the tranquilizers would be better than having an ill-tempered wolf clawing at my insides. Also, I had yet to hone my skill of reading minds and voices swam in my head constantly. Between that and my wolf, I was losing it. I'm not sure how I did it, but I willed my wolf down. She's stayed down for the past two years.

I look to the clock and only forty-five minutes have passed since I lay down. What I wouldn't give for a full night of restful sleep. I sit up on the bed and pull myself together.

"Open up," Ian bellows from the other side of the door, hitting it with his fists for good measure. I jolt from the sound. Damn, must be dinnertime. I open the door and meet his pissed-off face. "Are you ready?" he barks, eyeing me with disdain. He's told me many times that he's pissed he'll never find his true mate because of me. I sat there quietly during his words, but what I wanted to tell him was at least he had a choice in the matter. He's the one that agreed to do this to move up in the ranks. He could have taken a different route, but I kept my mouth shut because my words would have just added fuel to his fire, and I was not going to deal with him.

My mask falls into place. "Yes, of course." He holds out the crook of his arm and I place mine through the hole, hating even touching him.

'I cannot believe I am stuck with this shit for the rest of my life. Being by her side. What the fuck? Like my mate isn't out there. All this shit had better be fucking worth it.' His thoughts ring in my ears. He knows I can hear them, but he long ago stopped giving a shit. He can think what he wants; at least my thoughts are my own. No one can have those.

We enter the main dining room where rows of tables and chairs sit, along with a huge buffet full of food. No one utters a word to us as Ian lets go of my arm and we get in the buffet line. I gather some lettuce, tomatoes, cheese, and crackers and walk over to our spot at the table. This is not a *come sit where you want and be comfortable* room. No, this is a formal, *sit in your spot, no questions asked* kind of room. Ian slides in next to me, his plate loaded with meats, and my stomach rolls. I push my fork into the lettuce, then place it in my mouth and try to choke some of it down. I'm not sure what happened to me all of that time I was locked up, but something inside of me changed. From when I got out and to this day, I have a very difficult time keeping anything down.

A plate is slid in front of me from the other side of the

table. Roast beef. "Eat that. You haven't been eating right," my mother states like she actually gives a damn. She didn't care for years and now she wants to care.

"Yes, Mother," I say respectfully and pull the plate in front of me, even though my stomach protests. I force down the entire plate, wiping my lips when I'm finished. My body immediately wants to expel the food, but I do my damnedest not to let it.

Conversation carries between the wolves. None of it involves me so I don't bother listening. Anyway, if I wanted to know, I could go into their thoughts and find out. But I don't care. Alpha sits at the head of the table with my mother at his side, ever the stoic wife. They make me sick, pretending to be a happy couple. I can smell they are mates, but I've always wondered if my mother had a choice, what would she choose? It doesn't matter.

"So, did you hear?" Lisa, a female wolf, states loudly from the other side of the table as I go back to my salad. Why her voice catches my attention, I don't know. Normally I tune everything out. "Melody found her mate!" she squeals. My food rumbles again. I swallow. Mate. The hollow black abyss of my despair opens wide, swirling like a tornado threatening to suck me in. There have been so many times when I wished it would, but it doesn't, only leaving me with an ache so deep inside my chest that it's physically painful.

'Hopefully that little bitch heard that.'

Lisa's thoughts come through loud and clear. She's always been a bitch, but since Ian decided to tell her that we are not really mates, she is an even bigger one. When he told me, I stood there shocked as hell. He must trust her to give away that big of a secret because if Alpha finds out, I'm sure Ian will be dead.

Lisa hasn't yet mated with anyone, but she finds it prevalent to discuss these things at the dinner table, knowing and liking that it gets to me. After all the excited yelps from the pack, things settle down.

"Did you hear that?" Lisa states and I don't look up; surely, she isn't talking to me. "Hello, Zara I'm talking to you," her catty voice calls out. I breathe in deep, not allowing any emotion to seep through.

"Yes, Lisa. That is wonderful news." I dig into my salad and put a bite into my mouth, praying it will go down.

"Isn't it fantastic that everyone is finding their true mates?" She claps her hands in rapid secession, happy as all get out. '*Suck on that one.*'

Boy I'd love to lay into this bitch and tear her throat out. I'd never get that far though. I'd be pulled away because I'm too *useful.*

"Yes, it is." And isn't it sad that you haven't found yours, you conniving piece of shit.

"Melody is already planning the claiming ceremony and it's going to be grand." Oh sweet Heavens, here it comes. "You'll be there, right?" Like I could be anywhere else. Melody is a member of our pack and one of Lisa's many followers. Too bad she's losing one of her minions. Also too bad that if she joins whatever pack her mate is in, the family she grew up with will probably wipe her out. Pathetic.

"That will be up to Alpha," I reply in the same damn tone I hate.

"You will be required to attend," Alpha states from the end of the table. No doubt he wants to rub the mating in my face, too. Show me just how wonderful it would be to have found my true mate. He's made me go to all of them since agreeing to his terms. Each time, I just stand there, and then

I leave as soon as I'm allowed. I suck it all in, but never allow anything on the outside to show.

"Thank you, Alpha. I will be there, Lisa." She squeals again like a pig in a puddle. Inside, I'm rolling my eyes. Outside, I'm blank.

"Great, maybe Alpha will *let* you help out." '*Make you suffer some more, you bitch.*' Suffer. Didn't I already do enough of that? I have no mate to find. I have nothing. I *am* nothing. So why put me through more of nothing when I don't give a shit. I never got hate from my pack growing up. It didn't start until I got out of the cage and no one said a word to me as to why. I didn't even bother to ask or dig in their heads because I was past the point of caring.

"She will not be able to. She has work to do," Alpha announces. I don't know what's worse, doing his *work* or being around a bunch of giddy girls as they are decorating for a celebration and all the while rubbing salt in my gaping wound. Kind of a tossup really.

I say nothing. When Alpha excuses himself from the table taking Gregor, Ian, and some others with him, I leave, keeping my eyes focused ahead on the exit. I slam the door, run to my bathroom, and everything in my stomach makes its way into the toilet. I allow the tears to fall.

Read more in The Raber Wolf Pack HERE

CPSIA information can be obtained
at www.ICGtesting.com
Printed in the USA
LVOW11s0622180917
549104LV00001B/4/P